"Don't tell me you don't know!"

Jordan's voice was cold. "You're getting married next week—to the man you've already divorced—and you don't know about it?"

Next week. She was supposed to become Russell's wife *next week*. For the second time. He'd left her no choice. But it was the furious man standing before her that she loved.

"Well, say something, Willow," Jordan snapped. "Even if you only tell me it's true."

Willow swallowed hard but didn't speak.

"I think I have my answer now," he said quietly. "But why, Willow? You don't love him."

"Jordan, I think this is between Russell and me," she whispered.

"Last night changed all that!"

CAROLE MORTIMER, one of the most popular—and prolific—English authors, began writing for the Harlequin Presents series in 1979. She now has more than forty top-selling romances to her credit and shows no signs whatsoever of running out of plot ideas. She writes strong traditional romances with a distinctly modern appeal, and her winning way with characters and romantic plot twists has earned her an enthusiastic audience worldwide.

Books by Carole Mortimer

HARLEQUIN PRESENTS

HARLEQUIN SIGNATURE EDITION

Don't miss any of our special offers. Write to us at the following address for information on our newest releases.

Harlequin Reader Service
901 Fuhrmann Blvd., P.O. Box 1397, Buffalo, NY 14240
Canadian address: P.O. Box 603,
Fort Erie, Ont. L2A 5X3

CAROLE MORTIMER

velvet promise

Harlequin Books

TORONTO • NEW YORK • LONDON
AMSTERDAM • PARIS • SYDNEY • HAMBURG
STOCKHOLM • ATHENS • TOKYO • MILAN

For John,
Matthew and Joshua

Harlequin Presents first edition June 1987
ISBN 0-373-10989-X

Original hardcover edition published in 1986
by Mills & Boon Limited

CHAPTER ONE

'*DANI*, I don't think——' Willow's laughing refusal to let her four-year-old daughter sample her wine came to an abrupt halt as she found her gaze drawn and held by the man just entering the dining-room, the hand she had raised to prevent Dani lifting the glass to her mischievously quirked mouth faltering and falling, the colour draining from her finely etched cheeks.

Jordan St James. She had known a member of the family would call on her sooner or later—after all, that was the reason she had informed them of her visit in the first place. But they had only arrived this afternoon from London, and she had expected a little more time to settle in to the hotel and reacquaint herself with Jersey, the largest of the Channel Islands, before having to confront any of Russell's family. She should have known that the arrogant man rapidly approaching their table wouldn't wait for her to go to them!

'Oh, Mummy, it's—ugh!' Dani began to choke as the wine she had sipped in that moment of her mother's preoccupation hit the back of her throat, her pretty face suffused with colour, her eyes beginning to water. 'Mummy!' she protested, blinking rapidly as her throat seemed to be on fire.

'Darling, I asked you not to.' Willow took the

7

glass out of the tiny hand next to hers as it wobbled precariously, patting her daughter gently on the back as the alcohol took her breath away.

'What seems to be the trouble?' enquired the silky voice that Willow recognised all too well.

She only half-turned to acknowledge Jordan's presence beside their table, just the brief glimpse she had had of him as he entered the room was enough to convince her he was as imposing as ever, the darkness of his hair gleaming ebony in the light given off by the overhead chandeliers. He had been too far away at the time for her to see the brown velvet of his eyes, but she did know their velvety softness was a deception, that this man was capable of verbally ripping a person to shreds while his eyes maintained their brown velvet warmth.

'She's all right now,' Willow dismissed his concern, handing Dani a glass of water to wash away the taste she was now proclaiming as 'awful'. 'I did try to warn you, Dani.' Her voice softened noticeably as she spoke to her daughter, smoothing back the swathe of silky blonde hair from a face that was still flushed.

Dani screwed up her face. 'Are you feeling ill too, Mummy?'

She gave a puzzled frown. 'What makes you ask that?'

Her daughter grimaced. 'Because the wine tastes like medicine!'

Willow held back her smile with effort, although she doubted Jordan St James found the remark as amusing; he rarely seemed to smile, and she had never seen him laugh. 'I should stick to lemonade until you're as old as Mummy,' she advised gravely. 'Then the wine won't taste like medicine.'

Now that her choking fit seemed to be over Dani was taking an interest in the tall, dark man who stood beside their table, oblivious to the curious looks he was receiving from the other guests who had chosen to eat in the relaxed elegance of the hotel restaurant. But that was typical of the Jordan she remembered; he had so much arrogant self-confidence she didn't think he noticed other people's reaction to him most of the time. The hovering waiters were certainly aware of the prestigious identity of her visitor.

Dani looked up at him with candid green eyes. 'You look like the photographs of my daddy,' she stated quizzically.

Willow gave a start of surprise, turning to look fully at Jordan for the first time. Maybe he and Russell were a little alike: both very tall and dark, their facial characteristics slightly similar, although considering their relationship that wasn't so surprising. But the similarity was only slight; Russell was a much weaker version of Jordan St James visually, not quite as tall, nor as muscular, his face possessing none of the strength of character stamped so markedly on the other man's, although for sheer fashionable handsomeness most women would probably consider Russell the more attractive of the two, Jordan's features being ruggedly harsh rather than classically handsome.

Jordan smiled down at Dani, the dark eyes compelling. 'That's because he and I are cousins.'

Looking as harshly forbidding as he did, Jordan's voice should have been harsh too, but it was as velvety as his eyes, possessing a mesmerising quality that sent a shiver down Willow's spine.

'Really?' Dani brightened at this disclosure. 'Do you know——'

'Ah, Barbara.' Willow looked thankfully at the other woman who was now hovering behind Jordan trying to attract her attention. 'Could you take Dani up to our suite for me now?'

'Oh, Mummy, do I have to?' her daughter predictably protested. 'I'm not a bit tired and I——'

'Danielle Stewart, you've done nothing but yawn since we got down here,' she cajoled. 'Now go along with Barbara. And behave yourself— we're all tired and it's been a long day.'

'Do I have to?' Dani wheedled again.

Her expression softened at her daughters petulant face, a sure sign of tiredness in her usually sunny-faced daughter. 'You have to,' she told her firmly. 'I'll be up in a few minutes,' she promised as Dani reluctantly stood up to join Barbara.

She watched her daughter's progress out of the dining-room, all the time conscious of Jordan's ominous presence beside her. But as the animatedly talking Dani left the room at Barbara's side she had no choice but to turn and face him. It wasn't easy. 'Won't you join me?' She extended a slender hand to the seat opposite her that Dani had just vacated.

He gave an abrupt inclination of his head. 'She's very like you,' he rasped as he folded his long length down into the chair.

'Yes,' she acknowledged curtly, sure that the whole of Russell's family would have preferred it if Dani had looked nothing at all like the outsider who had dared to marry him.

Jordan's eyes narrowed at her resentment. 'That wasn't meant as a criticism.'

'No?' she scorned.

'No. You're a very beautiful woman,' he stated in a flat voice.

She knew that he wasn't trying to be polite or insincere, that Jordan St James only said what he believed to be fact.

When she had first met this man she had been a wide-eyed innocent with flyaway blonde hair and only a gauche charm at best, but the years of being Mrs Russell Stewart had at least enabled her to attain a veneer of sophistication, to wear only the best clothes, to have her hair styled in such a way it wouldn't dare be flyaway. Yes, over the years she had at least taken on a surface self-confidence; it was only when she was confronted with Russell's family that it began to crumble and leave her as vulnerably open as she had been at seventeen.

Jordan relaxed back in his chair, waving aside the waiter's suggestion that he join Willow for coffee; the dark suit he wore was tailored to the raw masculinity of his body, a brown tie knotted neatly at the throat of his cream shirt. The darkness of his hair was lightly sprinkled with grey at his temples on closer inspection, reminding Willow that he had recently entered his thirty-eighth year. Although he had never looked young to her, and Russell had often taunted that Jordan had been born old.

Orphaned at only five years old, Jordan had been taken into the home of his father's sister, Simone Stewart, and her husband David, and he and Russell had been brought up as brothers. The sibling rivalry Russell felt for his cousin didn't seem to be echoed by this self-contained man.

'However,' he added softly, 'beautiful women do not always make the best mothers. They have so many other—interests.' He met her gaze blandly as the force of his insult made her gasp.

From the moment they had first met just over five years ago Willow couldn't remember one occasion when this man had gone out of his way to be polite to her. He had seemed to take an instant dislike to her, had only tolerated her at all because she was Russell's wife. But along with her maturity had come the belief that she was as good as—if not better!—than any member of this family, including the haughty man looking at her so coldly.

'No more so than any other single parent,' she bit out tautly.

He shrugged broad shoulders. 'Most single parents don't have the wealth that you do and yet still choose to go out to work,' he drawled contemptuously. 'How is your business?'

Willow felt her temper rising, knew that her eyes must be flashing like emeralds, natural colour highlighting her normally pale cheeks. 'Business is fine,' she snapped. 'And I don't go out to work at all; I do all my designing at home.'

'And who takes care of the shops you've opened as outlets for your designs?'

She shouldn't really be surprised that Jordan knew so much about her; Dani might only be a girl, and not the male heir the family had been hoping for, but she was the only grandchild the Stewarts had, and she had been put in Willow's custody. Even from the distance of Jersey the family would keep an eye on Dani, and, in doing so, a little on Willow too.

'I only have one in London, another in New York, and the latest one here in Jersey,' she dismissed tightly. 'And each of them is run by completely competent managers. If you're trying to accuse me of being a negligent mother then I think you should try again,' she challenged with resentment.

He raised dark brows over those velvety soft eyes. 'You don't think plying a four-year-old with wine at . . .' he glanced at the plain gold watch on his wrist, 'nine o'clock at night is negligent?'

She hadn't been plying Dani with anything, but she wasn't about to defend her action to this man; she no longer had to explain anything to him or any other member of this family. 'Which bothers you the most, the wine or the lateness of the hour?'

she taunted.

'Both!' he grated harshly.

She gave an impatient sigh and picked up her clutch bag. 'Dani doesn't exactly look or act like a deprived child.' She stood up, nodding her thanks to the waiter who had served her her meal, before walking out of the dining-room, tall and slender, the aquamarine of the gown she had designed herself a perfect foil for her straight drop of silver shoulder-length hair, its very simplicity of style giving it a colour and texture that had been lacking when it hung in a straight swathe to her waist. Besides, that other style had given her the look of Alice in Wonderland, and with the birth of her daughter she had become very much a woman.

She had reached the bottom of the elegantly curved staircase before she felt the firm grasp of steady fingers on her wrist. From her advantage of already being two stairs up she turned and found herself on an eye-level with Jordan for the first time, the effect of those warm brown eyes even more devastating. Her breath caught in her throat as she felt the first stirrings of feminine interest in a man she had known for a long time. A very long time.

Her initial reaction to that interest was panic, and she pulled her hand out of his grasp as his eyes narrowed at the action. 'I've arranged to take Dani over to see her grandparents tomorrow afternoon,' she told him forcefully. 'I really don't see the reason for your visit here tonight.' Except to upset her. And he had done that!

He thrust his hands into the pockets of his trousers, pulling the material taut across his thighs. 'I was asked by Simone and David to see if you wouldn't reconsider staying with them instead of at this hotel,' he drawled. 'They only live half a mile away!'

After her divorce from Russell last year Willow had agreed that Simone and David should see their grandchild whenever it was possible for them to do so, and this business trip of hers to Jersey to check on her newest shop had seemed an ideal way for them to do that without causing too much upheaval in Dani's life. But when she had moved out of the Stewart home three years ago she had vowed to herself never to stay there again. She didn't intend to break that vow.

'The hotel is more convenient——'

'Than a luxury villa where you and Dani could have your own suite of rooms?' Jordan scorned.

That luxury villa had been her prison for eighteen months, with frequent visits from her jailer! 'We have our own suite of rooms here, Jordan,' she dismissed coolly, stepping aside to allow another couple who had just left the dining-room to ascend the stairs.

Jordan looked irritated by even that casual interruption. 'Let's go for a walk outside where we can't be overheard,' he suggested tersely.

'I have to go up to Dani,' she reminded him, shaking her head.

'Can't the renowned Miss Gibbons take care of her?' he taunted. 'I thought that was what you employed a nanny for!'

Willow's mouth firmed. 'Dani will be waiting for me to tuck her in, as I always do.'

He gave a mocking inclination of his head. 'In that case I'll get myself a drink from the bar and wait outside for you.'

Willow glanced outside. On this late September night the sky was beautifully moonlit, adorned with a million stars that twinkled and blinked as a warm breeze blew off the sea. It was a night made for lovers to stroll along the golden beaches hand in hand. There had been many evenings like this when she had lived here so briefly, but she had never shared any of them with a lover. And somehow she didn't think walking on a moonlit beach with bare feet had ever occurred to Jordan!

She nodded coolly. 'If that's what you would like to do. I'll be several minutes,' she warned. 'I always read Dani a story last thing at night.'

'Aren't you overdoing the devoted mother act?' Jordan drawled in a bored voice.

'I *am* a devoted mother,' she bit out. 'Dani and I both look forward to this special time of night.'

'I'm surprised a busy lady like you can spare the time,' he derided.

'Jordan——'

'I'm sorry,' he drawled without any real regret. 'Be as long as you want with Dani; I'm not going anywhere but outside.'

Willow turned and walked away from him, deeply resenting his implication that Dani came anywhere but first in her life. She did work hard, she admitted that, this latest shop of her exclusive designs appealing to both the wealthy residents and visitors on this charming little island and proving more successful than she had ever envisaged. But her career in fashion designing hadn't succeeded at Dani's loss; she spent every available moment she could with her daughter. And if Jordan St James had known anything about her other than the black and white reports he obviously received on her he would have known that. But he didn't really know her, or about the things that had happened in her life to make her a woman of strength and character, a woman who at only twenty-three was one of England's most successful fashion designers while still managing to be what she loved best of all, an attentive and loving mother to Dani.

'Feeling better now?' she asked Barbara after letting herself into the suite.

'Much,' the other woman nodded. 'Jordan St James?' she sympathised as Willow still looked pale from her encounter with the man.

'Yes,' she grimaced, putting her bag down on a table. 'Dani in bed?'

The other woman nodded; a quiet capable woman of thirty-five, she had helped care for Dani the last three years. 'She's tired out,' she said indulgently, 'but she's determined to hear her story.'

Willow smiled at that, knowing from experience that no matter how tired her daughter was she wouldn't surrender to sleep until she had heard

one of her favourite stories, and it was no good
trying to cut the story short so that she got to sleep
quicker; Dani knew them all word for word! Not
that Willow minded; it was a time of day they both
treasured, a few minutes of peace and tranquillity
after the events of the day.

Dani sat up in bed as soon as Willow entered the
bedroom. She was small for her age but the
fragility of her appearance was not matched by the
exuberant way she approached life, her eyes
permanently agleam with mischief.

Willow sat on the side of the bed to hug her,
laughing as the small arms clung about her neck,
Dani collapsing in a fit of giggles as Willow tickled
her to attain freedom. It was a game they played
every night, but neither of them ceased to be
amused by it.

Dani sobered as she settled back against the
pillows. 'That man downstairs——'

'Uncle Jordan,' Willow put in quietly, having
no idea if he would welcome or disapprove of the
title when he wasn't really an uncle but a second
cousin.

'Mm,' her daughter nodded. 'Did I know him
when I was a baby?'

Dani was going through the stage of being
fascinated by the fact that she had once been as
small as the babies she saw in their prams when
they took walks in the park near their home. 'A
little,' Willow confirmed with a frown. 'Although
I don't think Uncle Jordan is all that comfortable
with little babies.' She knew she was being kind,

that Jordan had barely glanced at Dani until she was a year old and had been able to trample over his feet to get where she wanted to go!

'He seems to like me now,' Dani said consideringly. 'Does he live with Grandma and Grandad?'

Willow shook her head. 'He has his own villa a short distance away from theirs.'

'But——'

'Story-time, young lady,' Willow put in firmly as Dani's lids drooped tiredly in spite of her interest in her newly realised uncle. 'We can talk about Uncle Jordan again tomorrow.'

The expected protest was quickly forthcoming, but Willow soon calmed Dani down as she began to read her favourite story about a rather naughty bear. Unusually for Dani, she fell asleep halfway through the book, and Willow instantly felt a prick of guilt for having to keep her up so late after travelling today too. But Dani had napped at lunchtime before their flight, another unusual occurence for her, and so Willow had allowed the indulgence of the late night. And been soundly criticised for doing so! But criticism from Russell's family was nothing new.

'Still think it was a good idea to choose Jersey for your third shop?' Barbara looked at her concernedly as she returned to the lounge.

She grimaced. When the time came for a third outlet for her designs the natural choice had been Paris, but after careful consideration she had decided it was too obvious, and the feasibility report she had received on Jersey had been much

more promising: a lot of wealthy residents, and yet
only fourteen miles from France itself. She had
decided it was time to bury her ghosts, but she
hadn't realised at the time how difficult that was
going to be!

'I'm a businesswoman,' she stated firmly.
'Jersey was the perfect choice.'

'The Stewarts seem to think so to,' the other
woman drawled pointedly.

Barbara, who was as much of a friend to her as
she was to Dani, had been told from the first of
her connection with the wealthy and influential
Stewart family. 'Then I'll just have to disabuse
them of that fact, won't I?' Willow said determinedly, once again picking up her bag. She
smiled faintly. 'I don't have to ask you to listen out
for Dani . . .?'

'No,' Barbara smiled; the two women were in
perfect accord concerning Dani's welfare.

Willow paused after stepping from the hotel to
watch Jordan unobserved for several moments.
Several tables and chairs had been placed in front
of the hotel to overlook the bay, but Jordan had
forgone the comfort of them to stand by the wall
that fronted the hotel, his eyes narrowed as he
stared out to sea, ocassionally sipping from the
glass he held in his hand, his expression grim. He
looked even more forbidding in the moonlight, big
and dark, and infinitely powerful.

He slowly began to turn, as if sensing her gaze
on him, and Willow instantly moved forward
lightly, unwilling to be caught staring at him.

'Too?' he prompted abruptly.

She frowned her puzzlement, accepting the dry Martini and lemonade the waitress brought out to her, obviously at Jordan's request; it was her usual after-dinner drink. She was surprised he had remembered so unimportant a thing.

'Sorry?' She prompted an explanation to his question as soon as they were alone again.

'Dani asked earlier if you were ill too,' he reminded her grimly. 'Is she ill?'

Her brow cleared. 'Barbara had a migraine from the flight,' she explained. 'I thought it would be better if Dani and I had dinner downstairs together so that Barbara could sleep it off. It obviously worked.' Too late she realised she had excused Dani being in the dining-room with her that late at night after all.

Jordan's mouth twisted as he seemed to sense her resentment at the admission. 'She's feeling better now?' he drawled.

'Much,' Willow bit out, her hair gleaming silver in the moonlight. 'I believe you had some more things you wanted to discuss with me?' she pressed tautly, wanting this conversation over as soon a possible. And not just because she was tired.

'The same things,' he returned harshly. 'Do you realise the embarrassment you're causing Simone and David by choosing to stay at a hotel instead of with them at their home?'

Her head went back in challenge, the delicacy of her features clearly etched; wide green eyes, a small uptilting nose, her mouth at odds with those

fine features, full and provocatively pouting.
'Dani may be their granddaughter, but I'm not
related to them at all,' she rasped. 'And I have no
intention of letting Dani go to stay anywhere
without me.'

'You're their daughter-in-law!' Jordan's eyes
glittered in the darkness.

'*Ex*-daughter-in-law,' she corrected tautly. 'I'm
sure my staying here at the hotel can't be any more
of an embarrassment to them than actually having
me to stay *with* them! They never approved of me
as Russell's wife and I have no intention of putting
Dani or myself through the trauma of being a
"guest" in their home!'

'You never gave them a chance——'

'They never gave *me* a chance!' Her eyes flashed
in warning. 'Who do you think was the more
vulnerable, the wealthy Stewarts or the young girl
who married their only son?'

'Simone was upset with the speed with which
the wedding took place——'

'So was I!' She was so tense a strong wind could
have snapped her in half, her breathing ragged.
'But little things like pregnancy have a way of
showing themselves the longer you wait!'

Jordan's mouth thinned. 'You got your wealthy
husband, didn't you?'

Willow stopped breathing at the accusation. Oh
yes, she had got herself a wealthy husband, the
rich and elusive Russell Stewart, who had decided
he wanted her as his wife. But she had been three
months pregnant with his child at their hastily

arranged marriage in a London registry office, and neither Simone Steward nor any of her equally snobbish friends had ever let her forget the fact.

She drew in a controlling breath. 'I don't think the two of us resorting to insults is going to help ease the awkwardness of this situation,' she told him with a calmness she didn't feel.

'I didn't realise I was being insulting,' Jordan rasped. 'I thought I was just stating the facts as they happened to be.'

This man knew what he was doing one hundred per cent of the time, facts or no facts, and he knew he had been insulting her just now. And it was true, she had married a wealthy man, and her pregnancy had been the reason for the hasty marrriage. But Jordan was wrong if he thought she had trapped Russell into that marriage; *he* had trapped her.

'Only as you know them,' she said quietly.

'As they were,' Jordan hit out harshly. 'Russell was devastated when you left him and took Dani with you. The divorce almost finished him completely.'

She was well aware of Russell's feelings. Just as she was aware of her own. And her only emotion at the time of the divorce had been relief—and freedom. 'I didn't come to Jersey to discuss the past——'

'Why did you come back here?' His eyes were dark velvet.

'As you've already pointed out, I'm a business-woman,' she stated calmly, 'and this trip will combine business and Dani's visit to her grandparents.'

'I take it you will be attending this visit with her?' he drawled.

She gave him a sharply searching look. 'Of course. Is there some objection to that?'

'None at all,' he returned smoothly. 'How long do you intend staying on the island?'

Her mouth twisted at the bluntness of the question. 'Are you part of the same security that requires all visitors to the island to sign a police register when you book into the hotel?' she taunted.

'No.' His harsh tone told her he was far from amused. 'But you must have some idea how long you intend staying.'

Willow frowned. 'I'd planned to stay until Thursday,' she told him somewhat warily; what did it matter to him how long she stayed? 'I have a fashion show to finish arranging for early next month.'

'I see.' Jordan put down his empty glass on the table, his expression thoughtful.

Willow eyed him suspiciously. He seemed uneasy about something, and she had a feeling she wasn't going to like that something. 'Jordan, what is it?' she prompted nervously.

'Has the island changed much since you were here last?' he enquired lightly.

'It's as beautiful as ever,' she dismissed tersely. 'Now tell me what's wrong.' Because something definitely was!

He raised arrogant dark brows at the demand.
'Nothing is wrong.' He looked out along the bay.
'It's rare that I actually have the time to stand still
long enough to take in the beauty of St Brelade's
Bay,' he murmured softly. 'I forget just how lovely
it is here sometimes.'

As one of the numerous financial advisers on
the island, Jordan was an extremely busy man, the
island being a thriving financial centre with its
enviable rate of tax and other benefits. And yet
Willow wasn't sidetracked by his observations at
all, knowing he was keeping something from her.

'You may as well tell me, Jordan,' she prompted
tautly. 'If you don't I'll have to ask Simone,' she
added threateningly, knowing how all the men in
the family were protective of the tiny woman who
had somehow managed to conceal her steely heart
and determined nature from them all.

His mouth tightened at the threat, his eyes
narrowed. 'You're out of your league with me,
Willow,' he told her softly.

She didn't so much as blink at his tone of
menace, watching as a grudging respect for her
entered his eyes. He could keep his damned
respect; she just wanted some straight answers! 'I
mean it, Jordan,' she challenged.

'So do I,' he rasped.

A shiver of apprehension rippled down her
spine, but there was no outward sign of her
disturbed emotions as she continued to silently
meet his gaze, willing him to talk to her.

Jordan's gaze was finally the one to turn away.

'You've turned into a veritable tigress, haven't you?' he scorned.

'I've merely become a survivor,' she bit out.

He shrugged. 'It may not even happen. He's said he was coming before and then changed his mind without warning. Simone——'

'He?' Willow echoed sharply. 'You mean Russell, don't you?' Her unlacquered nails dug into the palms of her hands, her body rigid with tension. 'Are you telling me he's coming here?'

Jordan gave another dismissive shrug. 'He only said he might visit Simone and David some time this week; nothing definite has been planned.'

'Did he know Dani and I were going to be here?' she demanded to know.

'I doubt it, although Simone may have mentioned it to him. For God's sake, don't look so stricken; you were married to him once,' Jordan added disgustedly.

Russell. Here. Russell, with the laughing blue eyes, overlong dark hair, and with the body of a Greek god. It had been a year since she had last seen him, the first six months of that time spent expecting to see him every time she opened the door or turned a corner, the next six months spent grateful that she hadn't.

It was this last year of peace and tranquillity that had given her the hope he had changed during that time.

But maybe he hadn't.

CHAPTER TWO

WILLOW'S first instinct when she crawled out of bed the next morning after a sleepless night was to run, and to keep running. But she had done that when she finally managed to leave him, and he had only found her again, refusing to stay out of her life. Maybe it was time to stand and face him. She didn't really have any choice; she knew, for Dani's sake, that she couldn't keep running away from Russell. And maybe, just maybe, he would decide not to come here after all. It was a cowardly wish, but then she had never professed to be anything else.

While Barbara took Dani down on to the beach in front of the hotel, Willow drove into St Helier to visit her new shop, confident she could concentrate on business with the other woman in charge of Dani. The number of customers in the shop, despite the early hour, showed her she had indeed chosen well for her third location.

It was good to see Marilyn again; she had been in charge of the London shop until moving here; the two of them were old friends. For someone who hadn't been sure she could adjust to living on an island only forty-five square miles in size, Marilyn had adjusted very well, and was ecstatic about the beautiful weather and the friendliness of the islanders.

Willow enjoyed helping out in the shop for the morning, caught up with the last three months' gossip with Marilyn in between working, and was satisfied that everything was running smoothly there before she left shortly after twelve, sure that the new lines she would be introducing at the fashion show next month would go over very well here.

She had told Barbara and Dani that she would join them back at the hotel for lunch, and she was buoyed up with the success of her morning as she went down to join them on the beach, coming to a halt part way down the steps as she saw the dark-haired man sitting with them on the sand, with Dani chatting away to him as if the two of them were old friends.

Then the man turned, and Willow's breath left her body in a ragged sigh as she saw it was Jordan seated there. For a moment she had thought Dani was right, that Russell and Jordan did look alike from certain angles.

Jordan stood up as she approached them, brushing the sand from his hands as he did so. His eyes narrowed as his gaze moved searchingly over her deathly white face. He was dressed casually today, loose white trousers and an equally loose white shirt, the latter with its buccaneer style more fashionable than anything else Willow had ever seen him wear.

The white clothes looked magnificent against

his dark skin and colouring, and once again Willow was unwillingly reminded that he was a very attractive man. In the past she had always been too engrossed with being Russell's wife to really see Jordan in that way, but twice in as many days she had been made physically aware of him. She didn't like the feeling.

Jordan had never left her in any doubt that he regarded the majority of the female sex with contempt and, although he was sexually in the prime of life for a man, Willow had rarely seen him with a woman, let alone take one home with him. Russell had occasionally hinted at an unhappy love affair in Jordan's past, but she had never been interested enough to ask what it had been. Now she wished that she had. She had a feeling that with this man it was best to have all the aces in the deck.

'Mummy!' Dani's face lit up as she spotted her; she ran across the golden sand, silver braids flying in the warm breeze, to launch herself into Willow's arms. 'Have you finished work for today?' she asked hopefully.

Willow glanced at Jordan before answering, sensing his silent disapproval of the career that had taken her away from her daughter for the morning, the career he had said she didn't need. She turned back to Dani. *Did* she neglect this beautiful child in favour of her career? Trips like this one to Jersey were rare, as were the ones to New York, and Dani always accompanied her when she did have to go away, albeit in Barbara's

care. But she always took care of her business in
London while Dani was in kindergarten, her
designs usually being created when Dani was in
bed for the night.

No matter what Jordan thought to the contrary
she was sure she gave more of her time and love to
Dani than a lot of women in her position could, or
did. And there was always Barbara.

'For today,' she confirmed lightly, studiously
avoiding Jordan's gaze as she turned to admire the
huge sandcastle Dani had built during the morning, slipping off her sandals to dig her toes into the
sensuous warmth of the sand, knowing she looked
cool and comfortable in the emerald green
shirtwaister with its wide black belt. 'Everything
OK, Barbara?' She looked searchingly at the other
woman as she watched them from her sitting
position on the sand.

'Fine,' Barbara assured her briskly. 'Mr St
James has been helping us build a moat for the
castle.'

'Isn't it lovely?' Dani still clung to Willow's
hand. 'Uncle Jordan said he would show me a real
castle tomorrow. You have to walk out to it across
the sea, and——'

'The causeway is under the sea, Dani,' Jordan
corrected indulgently. 'You can't walk out to the
castle unless the tide is out; we have to use an
amphibious craft to cross before then. And I only
said we would go if Mummy agreed,' he added
with gentle reproof.

It sounded as if Jordan had been on the beach

for some time, building the moat and suggesting outings to Dani, and she couldn't help but feel curious about his motive. He had left her last night shortly after telling her of Russell's proposed visit to his parents; maybe Jordan thought she would go back to England before she had to face such a meeting, She certainly didn't relish the idea of seeing Russell again, but she had told Simone and David she would take Dani to see them, and she wouldn't go back on her word.

'Mummy?' Dani prompted worriedly at her mother's lack of response.

Willow smiled down at her daughter. 'I can take you out to Elizabeth Castle myself, Dani, if you would like to see it. I'm sure Uncle Jordan is too busy at work to take any more time off.' She looked at him challengingly, suspicious of his suggestion to Dani; he had never given the impression that he even liked children, and yet here he was making sandcastles and offering to take Dani out tomorrow.

He shrugged broad shoulders, the loose shirt moving against the strength of his body. 'The world of finance can do without me for a few days,' he dismissed. 'I'm sure Dani would enjoy the Castle.'

Willow couldn't stop the protective action of placing her hands possessively on Dani's thin shoulders, her daughter looked small and vulnerable in the red bathing costume that made her look all gangling arms and legs. 'As I said, if she wants

to go I'll take her. Or Barbara will,' she added
determinedly.

Brown eyes narrowed, but whatever Jordan had
been about to say remained unsaid as Barbara
suggested to Dani that the two of them go for a
swim in the sea. Dani ran off with a wild whoop of
delight, confident that the adults would decide
who was to take her to see the Castle, and Barbara
had to run after her to catch up with her before she
plunged into the cold water.

The warmth of love faded from Willow's eyes as
she turned back to Jordan. 'It was kind of you take
the morning off work to spend time with Dani.'
There was dismissal in her voice, and she knew by
the flash of anger in the velvet eyes that Jordan
had heard it—and didn't like it!

He thrust his hands into the pockets of his
trousers, heated anger emanating from his body.
'How was the shop?' he bit out.

'It seems to be doing well,' she answered, as
coolly as he, narrowing her eyes against the sun to
watch Dani cavorting in the shallow water.

Jordan nodded. 'I have several friends who said
they've shopped there.'

She turned to him with widened eyes; it was the
first time she had ever heard him admit there *were*
women friends in his life. 'At the moment most of
them are still curious to see the little toy Russell
Stewart's wife found to amuse herself with after
the divorce,' she derided. 'Let's hope they'll still
come in to buy once that curiosity wears off!'

He frowned at her self-derision. 'I'm sure you're

wrong about their motives. Your designs are
considered to be very fresh and feminine.'

'They are,' she said without conceit; every one
of her designs, but especially the evening gowns
she specialised in, was aimed at the softer more
feminine side of woman that had been lacking in
fashions of recent years. 'But I met several of
Simone's set there this morning, and they were not
just interested in the clothes!'

'You always did have this strange idea that
Simone's friends disliked you,' he dismissed with
ill-disguised impatience.

'Despised me,' she corrected hardly. 'The
daughter of one of Russell's own employees daring
to marry a Stewart!' She shook her head mockingly. 'They all expected some little country
bumpkin; and I certainly didn't disappoint them!'

It wasn't true about the 'country bumpkin'
image; she had never lived outside the hub of
London. But at seventeen, still a college student,
and so obviously pregnant, she had felt gauche and
unsophisticated when Russell had brought her to
his parents' home to live and introduced her to the
people who were his friends, and who would be
her friends too, now that she was his wife.

There had been little chance of that! She was
the daughter of a salesman, her clothes were
obviously made from inexpensive materials, even
though they were original designs she had made
herself. And she had known nothing of the
privileged life those people led, with their sophisticated parties and designer-label clothes. Their

morals could never be called sophisticated, only
alley-cat, and she had wanted no part of that
either. Although that was one thing Russell didn't
subject her to, making it obvious from the first
that she was his exclusive property. Everyone
thought it very amusing that Russell actually
seemed in love with his pregnant child-bride,
although it couldn't be said he had set a fashion, as
his friends continued their bedroom games.

'You were the one who despised us,' Jordan
rasped grimly, also seeming to remember that time
well. 'Looking down that turned up nose of yours
at the spoilt and privileged rich! How does it feel
to be one of us?' he taunted.

Her eyes flashed deeply green. 'I'm far from
being spoilt. And I'm certainly not privileged
either. I had to work, and work hard, for what I
have today.'

'That isn't what Russell's lawyer said after the
divorce,' he scorned. 'Russell gave you everything
you asked for, and more. The poor fool was still in
love with you then, wasn't he?'

Willow could feel her face pale. 'That's none of
your business,' she told him shakily. 'I don't
believe we've ever known each other well enough
to talk this intimately about our private lives.'

Jordan moved to stand in front of her, ominously close, his gaze moving over her contemptuously.
'Your marriage to Russell was never private,' he
scoffed. 'A couple of dates with your father's boss
and you decided you liked the idea of a rich
husband,' he sneered.

'Getting myself pregnant to make sure he had to marry me!' she returned heatedly.

'Exactly. Russell had never met anyone like you before,' he grated. 'A sweet innocent—little viper!'

She bit back the fiery retort that sprang to her lips. The things she could say in her defence she had no intention of telling anyone. Ever. Least of all this cold harsh man who was more like Russell's brother than his cousin.

'Your parents must have been delighted you managed to catch such a rich prize,' Jordan continued remorselessly. 'I heard your father is in charge of sales now rather than just another salesman.'

These were two accusations she could never deny. Her ambitious mother had been ecstatic when told Willow was pregnant by Russell Stewart and was going to marry him. And her father hadn't been able to believe his good fortune when Russell quickly promoted him until he reached the executive position he now held. Russell had bought them a new house too, in a more fashionable part of London, and even though he and Willow were now divorced her mother still called him their 'wonderful son-in-law'.

Jordan was quite right in his assumption of her parents' joy in her marriage, but she considered those things and the money awarded her at the divorce small remuneration for the price she had had to pay.

'You would have to talk to Russell about that,' she told him coldly. 'I see very little of my parents nowadays.'

'Slightly upset with you for divorcing the golden goose, are they?' he taunted.

The fact that he was right still hurt more than she wanted to admit. Her parents had never been interested in hearing the reasons she had finally divorced Russell; they were just furious about the fact that she had. She had wished then that she could have seen their greedy ambition when she was seventeen, that the years in between had never happened. But then she had thought of Dani, and realised that something good had come out of the marriage after all.

She shrugged. 'They still have the house Russell bought them, and my father still has his job.'

'That's because at the time of the divorce Russell still loved you!'

'I didn't want him to,' she told Jordan flatly.

Brown velvet eyes moved disparagingly over her face. 'I wonder what it was about you that so captivated Russell all that time?'

She had often wondered that herself—and wanted to destroy whatever it was! But she couldn't even be called beautiful, with her gamine features and fine hair; she possesed none of the flirtatious artifice that was supposed to keep a man enthralled and guessing. But Jordan was right, Russell had agreed to the divorce, while still loving her. She had hoped his absence from her life the last year meant that was no longer true.

'I have no idea,' she dismissed carelessly. 'Now, if you'll excuse us, Dani has to have her lunch before we go to see your aunt and uncle.'

'You always were so indifferent to the fact that Russell loved you,' Jordan said disgustedly. 'I've known Russell all his life, watched as women chased after him while he treated them with bored tolerance. And then at twenty-eight he met you, a girl of no more than seventeen, who treated him with contempt most of the time, with bored indifference the rest of the time!'

Never with indifference! If Jordan really believed that he was so wrong. Russell had been too demanding, too much in love ever to be ignored!

Jordan took her silence as confirmation of his accusation. 'You have the beauty of an angel, the body of a siren, and the heart of a bitch!'

Willow watched him as he strode away, her mouth trembling precariously as she felt herself on the edge of tears. In the past Jordan had had little time for her, and this was the first time he had let her know so verbally his real feelings for her. And he was wrong, so wrong. She didn't have the heart of a bitch; she didn't have a heart at all; that had been broken years ago by a man who had coveted it above everything else.

Dani was barely able to contain her excitement during the short drive over to see her grandparents. Simone and David had visited her several times in London, but this would be the first time

she had returned to their St Brelade's Bay home
since she was a year old. Willow had to admit she
was nervous about returning there herself. Simone
had always been polite when she had visited them
in London, but here on her home ground she might
not feel the need, and memories of past slights by
the older woman crowded Willow's mind as she
drove. David Stewart was a different proposition
altogether; very easy-going, totally dedicated to
the exclusive jewellery he sold here and in his shop
in London.

As they neared the house, Willow wondered if
she had been wise to let Barbara take the afternoon
off instead of accompanying them; she would have
felt more comfortable with at least one person on
her side.

She felt her trepidation grow as she saw
Jordan's dark grey Mercedes parked in front of the
low rambling villa that had a majestically beautiful view of the whole of St Brelade's Bay. The villa
itself was built of the local granite, as were most of
the other houses and walls on the island, the stone
coloured from pink to yellow and browns to pale
grey. It gave the modern structure an aged beauty
and grace that was usually lacking in new
buildings.

But the beauty of the house hadn't stopped it
becoming Willow's prison in the past, and she
trembled slightly as she and Dani entered the cool
interior to be shown into the sitting-room where
Simone and David waited for them, Simone
seated gracefully in one of the armchairs, David

slightly slouched on the sofa.

But is was to the tall man standing in front of the long window that Willow's gaze was drawn. He had changed into cream trousers and a brown shirt since leaving them this morning, and although he showed none of the uncharacteristic anger he had displayed this morning he didn't look in the least approachable either. It didn't seem fair that he had been blessed with those velvety eyes when he had a heart as cold as ice!

'Danielle!' Simone's still beautiful face lit up animatedly as she held out her arms to a Dani suddenly gone shy. At fifty-three Simone went to great pains to look at least ten years younger and, with the impishly curling black cap of hair and the slightness of build, she had no trouble doing so. Willow ruefully recognised the cream silk dress as one of her own creations. But she was conscious of the fact that even this concession to the career she had made for herself since leaving Russell might only be for show. Simone was a great one for maintaining impressions; her son might have made the *faux pas* of taking a pregnant child as his wife, but Simone would never let anyone outside the family see how much she had hated the marriage.

'She'll be all right once she gets used to you again.' Willow tenderly stroked the hair at her daughter's temple. 'She's been talking about you non-stop on the way over here,' she added hastily as the blue of Simone's eyes flashed resentfully at the implication that Dani regarded them all as strangers. But it had been several months since Dani had seen her grandparents, and to a child that could be a long time. Although she accepted that that wasn't Simone's and David's fault; she had never been able to fault them as grandparents.

'How about some ice-cream?' suggested David, a tall sandy-haired man of about fifty-five with twinkling blue eyes. 'We have chocolate, your favourite,' he tempted Dani as she hesitated.

'With a coloured cone?' Dani said eargerly, her shyness evaporating at the mention of the chocolate flavour.

'Pink or green,' he nodded indulgently.

'Green, please! Mummy?' Dani hesitated, looking at her uncertainly.

'Grandad made a lovely ice-cream cone,' Willow encouraged huskily, a lump in her throat as the two of them walked out of the room hand in hand, Dani telling her grandfather about kindergarten. Although their departure served to leave an awkward silence behind them.

'How are you, Willow?' Simone finally enquired coolly.

'Well, thank you. You?' Willow returned as distantly.

'The same,' the other woman drawled. 'Sit down, won't you?'

Jordan hadn't spoken a word since she and Dani had come into the room, and she glanced at him quizzically as she sat down. Why had he bothered to come here at all today if he was just going to stand there like some disapproving statue? Why *was* he here? He didn't live here any more, and she had presumed he would be going in to his office this afternoon after missing this morning.

'Would you like to go for a drive?' He spoke suddenly, his voice harsh.

'No,' she answered instantly, colour flaming her cheeks as she realised how rude that had sounded. 'Thank you,' she added awkwardly.

'Perhaps a walk in the garden, then?' he prompted again.

Willow looked at him with narrowed eyes, having the distinct impression that he wanted her to go out with him so that Simone and David could be alone with Dani. 'No—thank you.' This time the latter came out drily.

'Really, Willow, anyone would think you didn't trust David and me to look after Dani for a few hours!' Simone snapped.

Willow calmly returned the other woman's fiery gaze. 'It isn't a question of trust, it's just that Dani is still shy with you and David. Another time perhaps,' she dismissed.

'God, how you enjoy having the power to say whether or not we may see our own grandchild! You——'

'Simone!' Jordan cut in warningly.

Simone stood up. 'I trust neither of you has any objection if I join David and Dani in the kitchen!'

Willow knew that it wasn't a statement that required an answer. She put her hands demurely on her lap, feeling the electric tension emanating

from the man across the room. Obviously he
disapproved of the way she had blocked Dani
being alone with her grandparents. At least she
had her answer as to what he was doing here; he
was supposed to take her off somewhere so that
Simone and David spent some time alone with
Dani. She had no intention of letting that happen.

'They love her a great deal, you know,' Jordan
rasped in the silence.

She sighed. 'I do know.' She gave an inclination
of her head.

'Then why did you——'

'Jordan, Dani is only four; at least give her the
chance to relax with them before trying to drag me
off out of the way!' She looked at him
challengingly.

An angry flush darkened his cheeks. 'OK, so we
weren't very subtle.' He sighed, moving forward
into the room. 'They only want Dani to like being
with them.'

'Without my influential presence,' she said,
deriding their tactics.

'You and Simone never did get on, and Dani is
bound to pick up on that eventually.'

'Can I help it if my most pleasant memory of
Simone is her assuring me that no one would dare
to slight me in her presence!'

'She was trying to be kind!'

'She was implying that her snobbish friends had
a *reason* to slight me!' Willow snapped heatedly.
'As if I cared for the opinion of any of them!' She
tossed her head back angrily.

'You made it very obvious from the first that you didn't,' Jordan told her quietly.

She gave him a sharp look. 'You make it sound as if it were my fault they were all sweetness and understanding in Simone's presence and bitchy cats behind her back!'

'Maybe it was, partly. You treated us all with contempt, and——'

'Oh, I've had enough of this particular argument!' She stood up agitatedly. 'I think I would like a walk in the garden after all.'

Jordan looked at her silently for several tension-filled moments and then gave an abrupt inclination of his head. 'Very well. If we go out through the kitchen we can tell Dani where you are.'

Willow was very disturbed by this constant bickering with Jordan every time they met. They had never argued in the past, had rarely found occasion to talk then, let alone argue. It was very disconcerting to find an adversary where before there had only been indifference.

'I'm sorry.' Jordan spoke curtly once they were outside in the sun-filled garden, Dani inside enjoying herself as the centre of her grandparents' attention. 'I'm prying into something that's none of my business. As you've already pointed out so clearly,' he added with self-derision.

She glanced up at him, once again shocked by the awareness of him that was the last thing she wanted in her life. Now, or ever. Russell had been enough to last her a lifetime.

'Have you heard any more from Russell about

his plans?' she asked as casually as she felt able to when discussing seeing her ex-husband again for the first time in a year.

'No,' drawled Jordan. 'But then we didn't expect to; he'll arrive when and if he feels like it.'

Yes, that sounded like Russell. He had continued to do the same thing in her life even after she had left him; was always full of demands. This last year of silence had been as unsettling as it was calm and tranquil, like waiting for an axe to drop. Even now Russell was keeping her guessing.

'Do you see much of him in London?' Jordan asked casually, and yet she sensed a real underlying interest in her answer.

She looked at him curiously as they strolled through the garden that was Simone's pride and joy, the wild display of flowers dominated by the pink trumpet of the famous Jersey lily, the blooms seeming to grow indiscriminately when actually Simone spent hours out here achieving just that effect.

'Nothing at all since the divorce,' she answered slowly. 'Why the interest?'

He raised dark brows at her defensive attitude. 'Dani mentioned that I looked like photographs of her father.' He shrugged. 'It seemed a strange thing to say if she sees him very often.'

'Russell is at liberty to see Dani any time he chooses to——'

'Will you stop taking every remark as an insult or a personal slight!' Those velvet eyes darkened. 'I only wondered at the remark.'

She sighed at her fiery response to what was just curiosity, after all. 'Russell hasn't asked to see Dani since the divorce, and children forget so easily . . . She has a photograph of him next to her bed.' She shrugged.

At first she had worried about Russell's lack of interest in the child she had given birth to only six months after their wedding, but as the months had passed and Dani had easily adapted to not seeing the father she barely remembered, Willow had felt grateful for that lack of interest, whatever the reason.

'So he's finally stopped loving you?' Jordan watched her closely.

'I believe so,' she dismissed lightly, showing none of the relief she had felt when she realised that had to be the reason Russell no longer haunted her making demands, demands she had met each and every time he asked. 'Why are you asking these questions, Jordan?' she taunted. 'Did you think I might cause a scene when Russell arrives, is that it?'

He drew in a ragged breath. 'You're both adults; you'll have to work that out between you.'

They were both adults now, but she had still been a child five years ago, had been flattered by the interest of a man like Russell Stewart then. He had been eleven years older than her, too old for her, and her parents should never have encouraged the relationship the way they had. It had been too late for her by the time she realised her image of a romantic hero had been a false one as far as Russell was concerned; he was all too human.

'Then why the interest in Russell and me, Jordan?' she frowned at him. 'Don't your reports keep you up to date on my social life?'

His mouth tightened. 'If there are any such reports I haven't seen any of them,' he rasped. 'I have no interest in reading about your life second-hand. If there had been something I wanted to know about you I would have come and asked you!'

Willow felt that fluttering awareness that was becoming all too familiar when she was around this man. 'As you just asked me about Russell?' she prompted unsteadily.

He nodded coolly. 'I needed to know that he no longer loves you.'

That fluttering became a veritable surge. 'Why?' she croaked.

'Because that's the only part of your life that interests me.'

'I can assure you I have no intention of acting the "siren" where Russell is concerned,' she scorned.

'I think that's as well,' Jordan shrugged. 'The two of us have never found it easy to share anything, least of all the same woman's bed.'

All the colour drained from her face. 'What did you say?' she gasped faintly.

His mouth twisted in a humourless smile. 'I'm sure you heard me,' he drawled, coming to a halt as she faltered and stopped beside him. 'You see, that wasn't a rhetorical question I asked you this morning.' The leanness of his hands cradled either side of her face. 'I really do wonder what it is about you that so captivated Russell and made him such a lovesick fool. I mean to find out for myself.'

'You said I had the heart of a bitch,' she reminded him breathlessly. She had never seen him like this before, with that sensual tilt to his mouth, the warm masculinity of his body reaching out to her.

'With the beauty of an angel and the body of a siren,' he acknowledged huskily. 'And it's those two things I'm interested in,' he added mockingly. 'You'll never hurt me the way you did Russell because I have no intention of falling in love with you!'

Wide, panicked eyes searched the calm of his face, and she felt as if her air supply were being cut off. There was no longer disgust or contempt in Jordan's expression, just a burning curiosity to have his question about her allure answered. By taking her to bed!

CHAPTER THREE

'CAREFUL, Dani,' Jordan warned in a deep voice. 'You don't want to fall in.'

Dani turned to give him a mischievous grin as she skipped and jumped her way across the causeway to Elizabeth Castle off the coast of St Helier, the tide having gone down far enough for them to cross to the Castle this way, although water still lapped either side of the pathway.

Willow followed behind them reluctantly, not even the sight of how happy Dani looked as she bounced along in her green shorts and matching sun-top lightening her mood of despondency.

After Jordan's outrageous statement the afternoon before she had pulled out of his grasp and run into the house, sticking close to the others until Jordan had left a short time later. She had intended to continue avoiding him for the rest of her stay here, but as she and Dani had been getting ready to go out this afternoon he had knocked on their door with the announcement that he was taking them both to Elizabeth Castle. Dani had been overjoyed, Willow just felt ill.

She still didn't feel too well, although Jordan's politely solicitous manner could in no way cause offence. But she couldn't just put from her mind the things he had said to her, and she looked at

48

him with totally new eyes as she realised he was
probably a very beddable man. If she had been
interested in going to bed with one. Which she
wasn't.

But that new awareness she had had for him
rang like an alarm bell in her mind now; she had
shunned even the most casual of contact with him,
ignoring the speculation in his eyes as she had
avoided the hand he had held out to her as she had
stepped from the car.

'Dani!' she warned as her daughter splashed
into a puddle and wet the bottom of the wheat
coloured trousers Jordan wore with a loose-knit
top the same colour as his eyes. 'Uncle Jordan told
you to be careful,' she reminded her irritably,
knowing she was taking out her sleepless night on
Dani, but unable to stop herself.

'Sorry.' Dani looked at her uncle sheepishly,
instantly forgetting not to run or jump as she
landed in yet another puddle.

Jordan dropped back a step as Dani went on
ahead, he and Willow walking side by side now.
'You seem a little tense today.'

Her eyes flashed as she glared up at him. 'I
wonder why!'

He gave a rueful grimace. 'I thought it was the
done thing nowadays to talk about sexual intent?'

'Jordan!' She gave him a censorious glance
before looking anxiously at Dani to see if she had
overheard, but the little sprite was still jumping in
and out of puddles, totally innocent of the tension
between the two following adults. 'I certainly

didn't appreciate your candour,' she snapped at Jordan.

'Would you rather I hadn't mentioned the part about wanting you?' he quirked dark brows.

'I would rather you didn't feel that way at all!' she told him fiercely, feeling a little like the doe being sought by the hunter, not by the stag.

He viewed her vehemence with amusement. 'But I always have,' he murmured self-derisively. 'Ever since you first came here. But you were Russell's wife then, and carrying his child. And you also thought I was as old as Methuselah, with about as much sex drive! I don't think you feel that way any more.'

He was aware of that feminine interest that had come to her so unexpectedly!

'Do you?' he prompted huskily as her cheeks flushed fiery red.

She couldn't allow this to happen, daren't allow herself the luxury of being attached to any man. Because there was Russell; there always would be Russell.

She looked at Jordan coldly. 'The fact that I've now realised you aren't quite that old doesn't mean I suddenly want to go to bed with you,' she scorned. 'Just what do you think Simone and David would make of the two of us having an affair?'

'They don't have to know,' he grated.

'So it's to be an illicit affair too?' she derided with distaste.

'Not at all,' he rasped. 'You said yourself you

would be leaving in a couple of days; I could come and see you in London.'

'Aren't there any available women here so that you could save yourself all that expense and trouble?' she scorned.

'Willow,' he bit out forcefully,' 'I don't like being laughed at!'

'Then why don't you stop telling me jokes?' She looked at him challengingly.

His expression hardened angrily as he swung her round to face him. 'I've never found anything remotely funny about the fact that I desired my cousin's wife,' he snarled. 'I've only told you how I feel because I've always preferred honesty to the artifice of sexual games. But don't think that you can use that desire to play with me the way you did Russell, because I'm not in love with you the way he was. However, I do want you, and I can tell you feel something for me too!'

'Dislike!' she scoffed.

'Oh no,' Jordan derided with confidence. 'It's not dislike I see in your eyes at unguarded moments.'

'Jordan, think all the bad things about me that you want, accuse me of anything that you want to, but please,' she put her hand beseechingly on his arm as she looked up at him, 'please don't want me.' And don't make me feel for you what I've only ever known with one other man, she pleaded silently.

Puzzlement flickered in the dark depths of his eyes before he smiled, a humourless smile that

slashed deep grooves into the harshness of his
cheeks. 'I told you, I always have,' he drawled.
'And in my experience that isn't going to change
until I've taken you to bed.'

She was almost tempted to beg him to take her
back to her hotel room now and get it over with,
and then he would know how one man had ruined
her for all others. Almost tempted. But she was
still too shaken by Jordan's unexpected claim of
desire for her; she couldn't take any more pain
today.

'You——'

'Oh, look, Mummy!' Dani's excited squeal of
delight interrupted them as she stood watching the
amphibious craft go by loaded with passengers
who either didn't want to walk across or still found
the water a little too high for them. 'Can we come
back in that, Mummy?' Dani jumped up and
down. 'Can we?'

'I should think so. Jordan?' She looked at him a
little uncertainly.

'Why not?' he shrugged agreement.

After that Willow was careful not to let herself
be left alone with him, following closely behind
Dani as they explored the Castle on the pretext of
safety, although she knew Dani was sensible
enough not to go near any dangerous edges.
Jordan seemed to view her efforts with amusement, and once again she had the feeling of a doe
being hunted.

She soon forgot her nervousness when Dani
began to ask questions about the German fire-

control tower on the summit of the Castle, calmly explaining the occupation of this beautiful island in a war that happened forty years ago. Unfortunately the island still showed many of these signs of its occupation, visible reminders to the people who lived and visited here that they were very vulnerable, being only fourteen miles from the French coast. But to a generation you were trying to teach that wars and guns achieved nothing but the death of innocents on both sides it was difficult to explain why these relics had been left as they were, the part they had played in history having been totally destructive.

Jordan stepped in then, and Dani seemed to accept his statement that history was history, whether it was good or bad. Willow was glad of his help as her own explanation began to flounder.

'Where is Miss Gibbons today?' Jordan drawled as they waited for the return of the amphibious craft.

'Back at the hotel, probably.' She frowned at his curiosity. 'Why?'

'I wanted to be sure you had a babysitter for tonight before I asked you out to dinner,' he told her.

And she had walked right into the trap he had set for her! 'Ask implies an invitation,' she told him coolly. 'And the answer is no. Thank you.'

'Frightened?' he mocked.

'Terrified,' she drawled in a bored voice that implied the opposite.

His mouth quirked. 'What's wrong with a little

harmless flirtation?'

This man had never flirted in his life, and if he had it had never been harmlessly. And she had never learnt how. 'I really don't have the time for this, Jordan,' she dismissed impatiently. 'I've been working for months to get my new lines for the fashion show ready for next month, and these few days away were supposed to be a rest before the chaos begins.'

'If it's so much work why do it? You have the shops,' he shook his head.

'It's expected of the top designers,' she said without conceit.

He studied her with narrowed eyes. 'You do look a little tired.'

Willow gave a disbelieving snort. 'You don't think that could be the strain of having you declare your intention of trying to get me into bed?'

He laughed. He actually laughed! And it was the most melodious sound Willow had ever heard. His eyes stayed the warm colour of soft brown velvet, crinkling up at the corners, his teeth white and firm against the sensuous curve of his mouth. If she weren't careful she might actually find herself liking this man, even though he believed she had deliberately got herself pregnant to entrap a rich husband!

Russell. Like the shadow he had always been lurking in her life, thoughts of him came along to spoil her day even more. So charming and debonair, yet he had deliberately destroyed her feelings for him with a vicious act of cruelty she would never forget. It was because of him she knew she would never love another man.

Jordan watched the pain flicker in and out of her eyes. 'Hey, it isn't that bad,' he chided drily.

She looked at him dazedly, not even realising who he was for a few seconds, shaking off the darkness of her memories as she heard the return of the amphibious craft.

She was aware of him watching her on the drive back to the beach, but the craft bumped about so much on the rocky sea-bed that she and Dani spent the whole time laughing as they bounced up and down on their seats, her gaze deliberately blank when she chanced to look at Jordan. The past was behind her now, and it had to stay that way.

'I'll pick you up about eight o'clock,' Jordan told her as Dani went off with Barbara to join the other children for the early tea the hotel provided.

'No.'

'No?' He quirked dark brows mockingly at her blunt refusal.

Willow sighed. 'I've arranged to eat at the hotel every night,' she refused again.

His mouth curved. 'They aren't exactly going to be empty if one guest decides to eat out tonight!'

Her eyes flashed at his derision. 'I like to be within calling distance if Dani should wake and need me.'

'My house is within calling distance, we'll eat there,' he told her arrogantly.

'I said no!'

'And I said yes.'

'Look, Jordan,' she snapped, angered by his calmness, 'we aren't teenagers, and I'm not the local girl all the boys have told you will give you a good time!'

His expression darkened. 'What the hell is that supposed to mean?' His grip on her arm prevented her walking away from him as she longed to do. 'Russell never discussed the intimate side of your marriage with me!'

'Nevertheless, I will not be passed from cousin to cousin like some toy you feel like playing with!' she hissed vehemently, very conscious of the fact that they were standing in the reception area of the hotel, with other guests walking past, two girls actually standing at the desk. 'You don't even *like* me!'

'I only invited you over for dinner, Willow,' he rasped, 'so that we could get to know each other better. No one mentioned going to bed together; I have a little more finesse than to jump on a woman the moment I get her alone!'

'Last night——'

'I gave you fair warning that I want you,' he acknowledged grimly. 'I also made it clear I could never fall in love with you. But that doesn't mean I can't come to like you. You made Russell as miserable as hell while the two of you were married, but I've learnt during the last two days that you're a good mother to Dani, that she obviously adores you as much as you love her. I've also come to realise that you *have* worked hard for the recognition you have in the fashion world. I still despise the way you tricked Russell into marriage, but I'm prepared to admit that I've been wrong about several of the other accusations I've levelled at you since you arrived.'

He was so wrong about so many other things too, but those secrets would be locked inside her for ever. 'That's very big of you, Jordan,' she scorned. 'But I don't want to be liked in spite of what I am. You see, I *know* what I am, and I really don't think it's that bad.'

'We'll talk about this more tonight——'

'We will not, because I'm not seeing you tonight!'

'Oh yes, you are,' he grated as determinedly as she. 'Be ready when I come for you at eight or I'll cause a scene like this hotel has never seen before!'

She glanced about them uncomfortably, aware that wouldn't be too difficult in this quiet elegance. 'That would only embarrass you.'

'And you,' he said with certainty.

She gave an impatient sigh. 'OK, dinner,' she accepted with ill grace. 'But I can assure you, you're going to be disappointed.'

'I'll be the judge of that,' he drawled.

You certainly will! Willow muttered under her breath as she joined Barbara and Dani in the restaurant. And to think that she had once decided that if Jordan had a sexual appetite it was satisfied quietly and discreetly. There was nothing quiet or discreet about his intentions concerning her!

She had never been to Jordan's home before.
There had never been any reason to in the past,
any family gatherings that took place being held at
Simone's and David's, Jordan living very private-
ly the rest of the time.

It was a beautiful house, more elegant, if not
quite as large, as Simone's and David's, with a
similar view over St Brelade's Bay. It seemed
rather a large home for one man, a man moreover
who seemed to be a confirmed bachelor.

She got even more of a surprise when Jordan
invited her into the spacious kitchen while he
cooked their meal himself, pouring her a glass of
wine to drink while he cooked thin strips of beef
with mushroom sauce, adding some of the wine to
the latter.

Willow watched him, fascinated with the
gracefully deft movements of his long sensitive
hands. He had beautiful hands, she realised for the
first time, only a sprinkling of dark hair on their
backs, the fingers long and tapered. They were
sensuous hands, the sort of hands made to caress a
woman, and Willow couldn't help wondering
what would have happened if Jordan had been the
man she had met all those years ago instead of
Russell.

The wine she had been about to swallow went
down the wrong way at the thought, and she began
to choke.

'Steady!' Jordan patted her gently between the
shoulder blades. 'Maybe you aren't quite old

enough for wine yet either, hm?' he said indulgently as she finally stopped choking.

She gave a rueful grimace, using a tissue to deal with the tears where her eyes had watered as she coughed. 'I didn't give Dani permission to sip my wine, you know.'

'I do know,' he nodded, going over to check on his beef. 'It's always been so easy to think the worst of you.' He looked at her consideringly. The fitted beige trousers worn with the short-sleeved cream-coloured shirt were tailored to him perfectly. 'I think we all forgot you were only seventeen when you first came here, no more than a child yourself and about to have one of your own. It may have been premeditated, but the pregnancy can't have been easy for you.'

Premeditated. She couldn't deny that, it had been deliberate. But she had been the victim, not Russell. He had seen the perfect way to make her marry him, and he had taken it.

'It wasn't.' The accusation went unrefuted. 'I had no idea you could cook,' she said interestedly.

Humour warmed his eyes. 'Oh, I managed to prop myself up against the stove once in a while,' he drawled. 'On the days I don't need the support of my canes, you understand.'

Willow gave a rueful smile. 'I never thought you were *that* old!'

'You make me feel it sometimes.' He frowned as he took two prawn cocktails out of the refrigerator to start their meal. 'Sometimes you seem so—new, untouched, and at others——'

'Prawn cocktail—my favourite!' she neatly cut off the insult she felt sure had been coming.

'. . . you have a maturity beyond your years,' Jordan finished drily, dark eyes mocking the assumption she had made. 'And I know prawn cocktail is your favourite; I asked Dani this afternoon.'

It was strangely domesticated to be sitting together so comfortably, drinking wine, eating the meal Jordan had prepared as they discussed Dani. It was a feeling that was totally alien to Willow.

'You're very eager to please,' she said sharply, disliking the idea of him asking Dani about her.

His steady gaze held hers. 'Always,' he murmured throatily, 'with a beautiful woman.'

Willow felt her breath catch and hold. Dear God, she had seen this man at least once a week if not more for the eighteen months of her marriage and never before had she been aware of him in this way. It made her feel threatened.

'I shall be taking Dani to see Simone and David again tomorrow,' she told him abruptly. 'And we'll be leaving on Thursday.'

'London is only a very short flight away,' he reminded her softly.

On a map Jersey looked so far away, seemed as if it should be part of France rather than England, and yet a flight that took only thirty-five minutes didn't make it seem very far away at all! 'I shall be very busy for the next few weeks.'

'Then I'll wait until the fashion show is over and you aren't quite so busy,' he dismissed, pouring her some more wine before going to serve their next course. 'There's no rush.'

If he had set out to deliberately charm her he had succeeded, Willow feeling quite mellowed by the good food and scintillating conversation by the time they went through to the lounge to have coffee, Jordan dismissing the need for her to do the washing-up, putting it all in the dishwasher.

'I grew up in a household run by servants,' he explained as he carried the tray of coffee through to the other room. 'Now it's nice to just have a cleaner in during the day while I'm at work and to do the rest myself.'

She understood what he meant, the numerous servants in Simone's household being something she had found very unnerving when she had first come to the island. She had never got used to their intrusive presence, kept her own house in London clean with the help of Barbara and Dani. But it was unusual for a man to be that independent.

Once again she found herself wondering if things might have been different if she had met Jordan first. They were discovering things they had in common, had discussed politics and religion during dinner without coming to blows, something even the best of friends were likely to argue about let alone two people who weren't quite sure of each other! But it was ridiculous to even think that Jordan would ever have noticed a seventeen-year-old the way that Russell had.

Russell. There he was again, shadowing an unexpectedly pleasant evening.

'Where do you go when you look like that?' Jordan probed softly.

Willow blinked dark lashes over pained green eyes, smoothing the knee-length silver and white gown down her thighs while she regained control. 'I was thinking what a delicious meal we've just had,' she invented.

His brows rose. 'Do you usually look sad when you've just enjoyed a meal?' he drawled sceptically.

'It's the thought of all those pounds I've put on.' She nodded lightly.

He didn't look convinced by the lie, but he didn't press her for the truthful answer. 'Is it still fashionable for women to be thin?' he grimaced. 'When are we poor men going to get a cuddly woman back in our arms?'

Willow's mouth quirked at his teasing. 'You look as if you've been deprived!'

He didn't return her smile. 'I've made love to a few women, women I've cared about if not loved. But I'm not a man who takes a woman to bed just for the sake of it.'

'I'll be a first, then,' she said brittlely.

'No.'

She looked at him searchingly, unnerved by the steadiness of his gaze. 'Jordan——'

'More coffee?' he enquired lightly.

Against all the odds, against her own feelings towards him, this man had drastically revised his opinion of her and was coming to care for her. She didn't want that. Russell would always come between her and any other man that she met.

'I think I should be going,' she decided firmly. 'Dani's inner clock is set for six-thirty, no matter what time her poor mother has managed to get to bed the night before!'

'It's only nine-thirty,' he drawled.

She knew that, but she had to get out of here. 'I've enjoyed the evening, Jordan——'

'You're acting as if you're afraid of me.' He frowned, his gaze fixed on her trembling hands.

One hand grasped the other to stop that tremor. 'That would be silly,' she dismissed.

'I agree.' He stood up, moving slowly across the room to sit beside her on the sofa, his body half turned to hers. 'I only want to caress and love every inch of you, not to hurt you.'

Willow felt as if someone had punched her in the chest and knocked the breath from her body as one of those leanly beautiful hands moved up to caress her cheek, his thumb lingering on her lips. There were flecks of gold among the brown as she looked into his eyes and she couldn't turn away again, drowning in that brown velvet as they beckoned, enticed——

She drew herself back with effort as she felt herself sway towards him. 'I have to go——'

'Not yet,' he said gruffly, his head bending towards hers. 'Oh God, not yet, Willow!'

She was prepared for an onslaught and felt only gentleness, a tender marauding of her mouth as his lips gave as well as took, bestowed as well as accepted, his mouth barely touching hers as he sipped from her.

If he had demanded or stolen from her she would have flinched away from him, but his very gentleness held her back from doing that, although she held herself stiffly, unresponsive, wincing as she saw the puzzlement in his eyes as he drew back to look at her.

'I know I didn't imagine that awareness between us . . .' he murmured softly.

No, he hadn't imagined it. But she had succumbed to that awareness once before in her life, had become a slave to the emotion. She wouldn't let that happen to her again.

'Is it Russell?' Jordan probed harshly.

It would always be Russell. Russell with the sensuously persuasive lips and the demanding hands.

'You're no longer married to him,' Jordan prompted impatiently.

In her mind she would always be married to him, always belong to him. The divorce was only a meaningless piece of paper that Russell would dispense with any time he chose to walk back into her life. He was part of her life that would never go away.

'Willow?' Jordan prompted concernedly at her continued silence.

She drew in a ragged breath. 'I don't want you, Jordan,' she told him truthfully.

A nerve pulsed in his rigidly held jaw. 'There's someone else?'

Russell. Always Russell ... 'Yes,' she confirmed shakily.

Jordan stood up forcefully. 'Why the hell didn't you tell me that in the beginning?' His eyes blazed. 'Or have you enjoyed watching me make a fool of myself the last two days——'

'No!'

'What was it, Willow? Retribution for all those slights you imagined you were given over the years?' He ignored her denial, glowering at her.

It would be so easy to say yes, to hurt him, and in so doing alienate him from her for ever. But she couldn't do it; she had never been the bitch he had presumed her to be.

She shook her head. 'I never pretended that I wanted you——'

'Then it was real!' he rasped, his eyes glittering darkly as he pulled her to her feet, grinding his mouth down on hers as he curved her body up into the hardness of his.

She should have felt revulsion, should have been cold in his arms, but to her stunned surprise she felt an uncoiling of physical response in the pit of her stomach, gasping her shock as she felt her nipples harden and thrust forward beneath the softness of her gown.

Since she had left Russell three years ago, men had swarmed around her, most of them for mercenary reasons, she felt sure, and it hadn't been all that difficult to avoid becoming involved with any of them. But Jordan was different.

She didn't understand, couldn't comprehend

her reaction to his brutality as her arms slid about his neck to pull him down to her, meeting the hardness of his kisses with a fierceness of her own, hungry for the passion she still sensed unleashed inside him.

'Don't play any more games with me, Willow,' he muttered as his lips moved moistly across the shoulder he had bared, the low-waisted silver-white dress having a high neckline and long sleeves but no back as it plunged in a deep V to the base of her spine, the material at her shoulders easily pulled down to bare her pointed breasts with their dusky-rose nipples. 'Let's just enjoy each other,' he urged as those pleasure-giving lips travelled across her throat and down to her breasts.

Fire surged through her body as she felt Jordan's lips and tongue tugging on her nipple with a pleasure-pain that made her legs weak. Her head fell back, thrusting her breasts forward, her legs buckling slightly as a thumb-tip rasped across her other nipple, as pebble-hard as its twin as it took its turn in Jordan's mouth.

'Beautiful.' His lips were slightly parted as he tasted her with his tongue. 'Made for love.'

Willow burned all over, felt giddy, weak, offered no resistance as she felt his hand move to the single large white button at the base of her spine that prevented the gown from slipping off her body altogether.

She could feel the pulsing hardness of his thighs, knew that Jordan was as wonderfully out of control as she was. And she knew he wasn't a man who lost control often. She felt a heady sense of power and exhilaration that she had been able to produce the effect.

'It will be good for us, so good,' he promised as he fumbled for the button on her dress.

She could feel him shaking with his need, put her hands behind her back to assist him.

'Oh, Willow,' he groaned, his face in her scented neck. 'Help me! Do—— What the hell?' He frowned as he raised his head, the flush of desire leaving his cheeks as he listened.

Willow listened too; she heard nothing at first, and then realised there was the sound of footsteps approaching the lounge where she stood so wantonly in Jordan's arms, naked to the waist, the thrust of her breasts hard and throbbing from the ministrations of his lips and tongue.

'Who on earth . . .?' Even as he questioned the identity of the intruder, Jordan pulled her dress back into place, his eyes darkening as his gaze swept over the pained bewilderment on her face. 'Willow, don't look like that,' he pleaded huskily. 'Whoever it is I'll get rid of them, and then we'll talk——'

'Well, well, well!' a mocking voice drawled. 'I hope I haven't interrupted anything.'

Willow's expression was stricken as she turned to face Russell. He looked back at her with cold blue eyes, the eyes of a man furiously angry, despite his slightly mocking tone.

CHAPTER FOUR

'WELL, isn't anyone going to answer me?' he taunted in their stunned silence.

Willow couldn't speak; her breathing was ragged, her palms damp. Russell looked the same as he always had, handsome in a way guaranteed to take a woman's breath away, his hair fashionably styled, blue eyes fringed by long dark lashes, his mouth sensuous, the expensive cut of his dark suit flattering his masculine build, a friendly questioning in his expression as he looked at them.

It was that very friendliness that made her nervous.

Russell had always said that he fell in love with her the moment he saw her meet her father at his office, had hated when other men so much as looked at her, and yet he now appeared to be taking calmly the obviously intimate situation he had caught her in with Jordan. It was a calmness that bordered on uninterest. If he no longer loved her, as she had suspected during the last year when she had seen nothing of him, then that would account for his reaction now. And yet she hadn't imagined that dangerous glitter in his eyes a few moments ago as he looked at them together.

'I was just about to drive Willow back to her hotel,' Jordan answered smoothly.

Russell glanced at his watch, his hands long and slender, almost artistic, although he had made his own personal fortune running his computer company. 'It's only ten o'clock,' he drawled sceptically.

His cousin shrugged, not at all disconcerted by the awkwardness of the situation. 'Willow was feeling tired.'

Chilling blue eyes levelled on her, and she felt her apprehension increase. 'I trust you aren't feeling unwell?' Russell prompted softly.

The situation was almost farcical, like some sort of drawing-room frolic, and yet Willow knew there was nothing in the least amusing about this. 'I have a headache,' she told him truthfully, a pounding in her temples, her unexpected response to Jordan forgotten in the shock of seeing Russell again.

'A walk on the beach should clear that,' Russell said harshly. 'I might as well drive Willow back, Jordan; it's on my way home.'

'I said I was going to do it,' rasped Jordan, his gaze intent on the pallor of Willow's face.

'That would be silly,' she dismissed lightly. 'As Russell said, it's on his way.'

The brown eyes narrowed angrily before he slowly nodded acceptance of her decision. 'I'll call you tomorrow,' he grated.

'Why?' Russell asked softly.

Willow watched anxiously as the two men eyed each other challengingly. Russell had been a baby of only one when Jordan came to live with them, and with a younger brother's jealousy he had always coveted that which Jordan wanted. But with Willow he had never had any reason to think Jordan would return the feeling, his expression darkening ominously at what he read in the other man's manner.

'I'm sure Willow appreciates your efforts to entertain her while she's here,' Russell drawled condescendingly, 'but she and Dani will be spending the day with me tomorrow.'

Willow's startled gaze flew to his face. She hadn't quite known what to expect from his visit here while she and Dani were here too; certainly not a cosy little 'family' outing together! 'It's been a very pleasant evening, Jordan, thank you.' She prepared to take her leave, stiffening as she felt Russell's arm go about her shoulders, withstanding the physical claim he was making on her as she smiled tightly at the granite-faced Jordan.

Surely this was the first time he had brought a woman home with the idea of seduction and found the woman taken home by his cousin! He looked far from pleased with the arrangement. But she could have told him he would be even less pleased with the scene that would have ensued if she hadn't agreed to leave with Russell.

Jordan stood in the driveway watching as Russell turned the car around.

Willow avoided his gaze, avoided looking directly at Russell too, although she could feel the anger emanating from him. And Russell angry wasn't something she relished dealing with just now.

'Have a good time?' he queried lightly as he turned the car out on to the narrow road.

'Pleasant.' She repeated her earlier description of the evening to Jordan.

'I've heard that Jordan can be very—entertaining,' drawled Russell.

She stiffened. 'If you have something to say, Russell, then I wish you'd just get it over with!'

He glanced at her coldly. 'I was merely asking how you'd enjoyed your evening with Jordan.'

He wasn't 'merely asking' any such thing. God, how she hated the games Russell played—she could feel her nerves stringing out tautly!

'You're looking good, Willow,' he rasped in the tense silence.

She swallowed hard. 'Thank you,' she accepted stiffly.

'Good enough for Jordan to want you?'

'Russell——'

'He does want you,' he murmured confidently, a smile playing about the sensuality of his mouth. 'Poor Jordan,' he derided tauntingly.

She bristled angrily, although she knew the emotion would get her nowhere with this man. And there was really no point to it; Russell was right in his assumption that Jordan's desire for her would never come to fruition. No matter how close she had come to surrender tonight! If Russell hadn't interrupted in the way that he had she knew that she would still be on her way home, that she

would never have gone to bed with Jordan. There
was no denying she had been aroused by his
caresses, but she knew herself well enought to
realise it would have gone no further than those
burning caresses.

'He doesn't seem to have realised yet that you
belong to me.' Russell's hand dropped possessively
to her thigh, caressing rhythmically. 'That you
always will!'

'We're divorced, Russell,' she reminded him
shakily.

His eyes glittered dark blue in the moonlight.
'That doesn't alter the fact that you're mine,' he
rasped. 'I never would have believed it of old
Jordan if I hadn't seen it with my own eyes. He
must want you very badly; he's never tried to take
anything that belonged to me before.' He gave a
speculative smile.

'He—Russell, you just drove past my hotel!' she
turned around protestingly.

'We haven't seen each other for a year, Willow,'
he reminded her softly. 'Surely you don't object to
my spending a little time with you now?'

It was what he did with that time that bothered
her, those old feelings of apprehensive tension that
had always been a part of her during their married
life together possessing her once again. In the last
year she had put from her mind just how knife-
edged life was with Russell, but this evening had
brought it all back with a vengeance.

'Besides, I promised you a walk on the beach,'
he added with soft intent.

Willow was instantly reminded of the fact that the other night she had realised she had never walked on the beach with Russell. How ironic that he should suggest they do so now. And she did have a headache, the fresh air would probably do her good.

He parked the car, taking off the jacket to his suit to throw it carelessly into the back seat, his shirt gleaming grey in the moonlight.

Willow trembled slightly as she walked down on to the sand beside him, wishing he would discard her as casually as he had the jacket, but knowing he never would.

The sound of the gentle surf on the sand filled the silence between them, although for Willow at least it wasn't a restful silence. Russell had come, as she had always known he would.

'Dani looks more like you than ever.' He spoke suddenly in the darkness.

She looked at him frowningly, her shoes off as she walked in the coolly soft sand. 'You've seen her?' she questioned guardedly.

He nodded abruptly. 'Miss Gibbons let me take a look at her earlier when I went to the hotel looking for you,' he explained.

Willow's mouth firmed, although she realised Barbara had had no choice but to acquiesce to his request; he was Dani's father, and that gave him certain rights. 'You could have woken her!'

'And ruined your pleasant evening with Jordan?' he mocked, bending down to pick up a pebble and skim it across the water. 'I don't think so, I was very quiet, and she seems to sleep very soundly. Does she ever ask about me?'

'Sometimes,' she answered curtly, not liking the idea of Russell going to her suite when she wasn't there. It made her feel threatened.

'And you?' He bent to skim another pebble. 'Have you missed me?'

She was glad of the darkness to partially shield her fiery cheeks. 'It would be impossible to be married to a man and then not think about him occasionally once you're divorced,' she answered with a tact she knew was essential with this man.

He straightened, moving silently across the sand to stand only inches in front of her. 'I said, have you missed me?' His voice was softly controlled, that very control making Willow wary.

He was such a handsome man, only thirty-three, and yet he wasted his life dwelling on a relationship that could never be what he wanted it to be. She had pondered the puzzle of the man many times, never coming up with a clear answer. Only Russell's desire for her had ever been that.

She moistened her lips with the tip of her tongue. 'I've—missed you,' she replied truthfully.

Desire leapt in the dark blue of his eyes. 'How much have you missed me?'

'Quite a bit,' she trembled as he caressed her cheek, the memory of another man's hand caressing her in the same way intruding on the moment, her eyes widening as she realised she was thinking of Jordan. Now, when she was with Russell!

'Show me how much,' Russell encouraged throatily.

Panic widened her eyes. 'Not here, Russell,' she protested breathlessly. 'We're on a public beach.'

'There's no one around to see us.' He shook his head, his hand moving to curve about her nape.

'But I—there's a man over there,' she noticed with some relief. 'Walking his dog.'

Russell gave the man a cursory glance. 'He isn't looking at us,' he dismissed as he turned back to Willow. 'And it's been a very long time since I held you,' he murmured throatily.

She knew how long it had been, she had counted the days, the hours, the *minutes*.

His expression darkened. 'Or has Jordan taken all you're going to give tonight.' His voice had hardened perceptibly.

She shook her head in silent denial, moving into his arms like a moth battering itself against a window pane, inflicting pain but caught in the light that commanded it.

Russell kissed her lingeringly, deeply, in no rush to end the pleasure, and Willow was clinging to him weakly when he at last raised his head.

His eyes glittered silver in the moonlight. 'No,' he murmured his satisfaction. 'You haven't given Jordan anything tonight,' he mocked knowingly, claiming her mouth a second time.

She swayed slightly when he released her, tasting him on her lips as she moistened them with her tongue. 'Why are you here, Russell?' she asked huskily.

'Surely that's obvious?' He shrugged off the question.

'Tell me.'

'To see you, of course,' he said impatiently.

It had been too much to hope that he had genuinely just been paying a visit to his parents. 'Why now?' she frowned.

'Why not now?' he derided.

Willow had always hated these games he played with her, hated the way they made her feel as if she had swum out of her depth and was floundering. 'It's been over a year . . .'

Russell grinned. 'I've missed you too, Willow,' he drawled mockingly. 'Didn't you think I would?' He quirked dark brows.

A nerve pulsed in her cheek. 'I didn't expect you to—completely drop out of our lives the way that you did,' she told him truthfully.

'You said you needed time,' he grated. 'From the marriage and me. I promised myself I would give you a year. That year came to an end yesterday,' he said with satisfaction.

He had 'given' her the year, a single year of sanity. Like a prisoner being given 'time off for good behaviour'. And she had been good, had always done everything Russell had asked of her. She had been a fool to think he would ever let her go.

Russell was watching her with narrowed eyes. 'I know there have been no other men during that time; I wouldn't advise you to start now, with Jordan,' he grated.

Willow's eyes widened as she realised Russell was the one who had had her watched, when all the time she thought it was Simone and David keeping an eye on their grandchild. She had the feeling of a butterfly stuck in a jar, still able to move her wings and fly, to watch the outside world, but allowed release only at the will and indulgence of her captor.

'I'd like to go back to my hotel now,' she told him abruptly, feeling a little sick.

'Exactly what I had in mind,' he purred.

Her eyes widened as she realised his intent. 'You can't stay there with me!' she protested.

Dark brows rose tauntingly at her obvious panic. 'I can't?'

She swallowed hard, hating having given him the satisfaction of seeing the emotion. 'Have you forgotten Dani and Barbara?'

His humour faded. 'I never forget about them,' he rasped.

'Then you must see——'

'Yes, I see,' he bit out forcefully. 'But *you* had better accept that I'm back in your life now. You've had the freedom you wanted, made a success out of your designing, now it's time for you to concentrate all your energies on me.'

Willow's breathing was ragged. 'Can't all this wait until we're back in London?'

'That depends,' he murmured softly, looking at her with narrowed eyes.

'On what?' she asked.

'On how successful you are at staying away from

Jordan!' His eyes glittered.

She sighed at the way he persisted in bringing Jordan into every conversation. 'We've had dinner together once——'

'Once too often as far as I'm concerned,' Russell snarled. 'He might not mind taking my leavings, but I would never accept his!'

She blanched at his crudity. 'There was no chance of that,' she gasped. 'You know that better than anyone!'

'Yes,' he acknowledged with satisfaction, his hand trailing familiarly across her breast. 'This has always been mine, hasn't it, Willow? Mine alone.'

She wanted to move away, to escape that caressing hand, and yet she couldn't, was once again that butterfly that could only be set free at its master's will. And Russell was in no hurry to go anywhere, his mouth trailing along her cheek to her mouth, his tongue moving inside its moistness in fierce possession.

His eyes gleamed triumphantly when he at last let her go. 'Until we get back to London,' he drawled.

She was shaking so badly by the time she got back to her hotel room that Barbara took one look at her and ordered her a glass of brandy to be brought up from the bar downstairs, not pressing her for any explanations until Willow had drunk it all down.

'I can't believe Mr St James would have——'

'It was Russell,' Willow burst out, looking up

desperately at the other woman. 'He came to Jordan's after he left here, and he——'

'It's all right.' Barbara took her in her arms, rocking her gently. 'We'll get through this together, Willow,' she comforted. 'We only have one more day here, and then we can go back to——'

'You don't understand,' choked Willow. 'He— oh God, he didn't say it in so many words, but I think he wants me to live with him again!'

Willow was composed but pale the next day, having slept badly, and wished she had the courage to leave the island today, before she had to face Russell again. It took no courage at all to face him; he wouldn't allow her to do anything else.

God, how she despised herself for her weakness, was filled with self-loathing as she made no attempt to even move her wings at her captivity. She had bruised and hurt herself too many times by fighting against that captivity.

'Willow, I—my God, you look terrible!' Jordan frowned at her as he seated himself across the table from her.

She gave a derisive smile. 'I doubt if that sort of flattery got you into any woman's bed!' Her smile faltered and faded as she realised what she had said, colour darkening her cheeks as she found she couldn't take her eyes off his mouth, those lips that had tasted and caressed her so intimately the night before. Jordan could never again be the coldly remote stranger he had always seemed to her.

One of his hands moved to grasp hers. 'What happened last night after you and Russell left?'

She drowned in the compassion in his velvet eyes, leaving her hand in his, reassured by the warm strength of his touch. 'We walked on the beach and then he brought me back here,' she answered huskily.

Those dark brown eyes narrowed. 'That's all?'

Willow stiffened slightly. 'What else did you expect?' she challenged.

He glanced about them impatiently; the dining-room was full of people eating their breakfast despite the lateness of the hour. 'Where are Dani and Miss Gibbons this morning?'

'Barbara took Dani to the playroom as soon as she'd finished her breakfast.'

'Aren't you feeling well?' Jordan frowned.

'I still have a headache, and I was a little late coming down this morning, that's all.' The sleeping tablet she had felt in need of the night before hadn't begun to take effect straight away, and when she had finally slept it had been so deeply she had found difficulty in waking up again. Dani, always ravenous in the mornings, hadn't been able to wait that long for her breakfast. 'Join me for coffee, Jordan?' she offered, wondering what he could be doing here so early in the morning. He didn't seem to be on his way to work, dressed in casual black trousers and a dark blue shirt. Hardly suitable attire for his exclusive office!

He shook his head. 'Let's go outside, the fresh

air might clear your head.'

It was a brisk September day, the sun shining but a certain coolness in the air, although there were several people on the beach taking advantage of the clear weather.

'Do you get these headaches often?' Jordan still maintained the hold on her arm he had taken as they left the hotel, his fingers light but unyielding.

Only when Russell's presence began to pressurise her! In truth it couldn't exactly be described as a headache, more an oppressive feeling. 'I'm sure it will go soon,' she dismissed. 'I didn't expect to see you this morning.' She turned to look at him.

'Why didn't you?' he grated, scowling slightly. 'I don't usually dine with a woman and then let another man take her home!'

'Injured pride, Jordan?' she derided with raised brows, feeling coolly comfortable in the loose cream blouse with its wide brown belt, the same colour as the trousers she wore.

His scowl deepened at the taunt. 'What really happened last night?'

Her expression was deliberately bland. 'I don't know what you mean.'

Jordan sighed. 'You told me the two of you were finished, and yet Russell seemed almost jealous when he saw us together.'

'He was understandably surprised,' Willow amended lightly.

'Why understandably?'

Her mouth twisted. 'You never even used to take the trouble to be polite to me, Jordan,' she reminded him drily.

His mouth firmed. 'Where do the three of you intend going today?'

She frowned, her brow clearing slightly as she realised he was referring to the claim Russell had made that she and Dani were spending the day with him. 'No definite plans have been made.' She shrugged. 'I expect we'll see him when we go to Simone's and David's.'

Jordan stopped his impatient strides, turning to face her, grasping her upper arms. 'Spend the day with me,' he urged, his eyes darkly compelling.

'I told you, we're going to Simone's and David's,' she said shakily, unnerved by his intensity.

'Willow, I don't like the idea of your being with Russell,' he told her roughly.

'Why on earth not?' she gasped.

'Before he arrived you were quite willing to stay in my arms!'

The fact that she knew he spoke the truth made her blush. She had only ever known one man intimately, and yet last night her reaction to Jordan had been undeniable. For that reason alone she knew she daren't risk being alone with him again.

'It would have gone no further than it did, Jordan,' she said confidently.

His eyes narrowed. 'Can you be sure of that?'

No, she couldn't be a hundred per cent sure, and her uncertainty must have shown in her eyes, and Jordan groaned low in his throat as he bent his head to kiss her. He showed none of the gentleness of last night, being demanding, a little rough, but her response to him was the same as it had been then; she melted into him as her mouth moved achingly against his.

He was in no hurry to end the kiss, relaxing a little as he felt her response, tasting her now, drinking his fill.

'How do you breathe when you do that?'

Jordan straightened ruefully to chuckle softly at the curiosity in Dani's voice as she stood looking up at them, a pretty little nymph in her bright red sundress. 'I think you're a little young yet for lessons in kissing.' He tapped her playfully on the nose. 'Ask me again when you're as old as your mummy.'

'I'm so sorry!' A slightly breathless Barbara reached Dani's side. 'She saw you both just as we'd crossed the road to the beach and I didn't get a chance to stop her.' She grimaced.

Willow's cheeks were fiery-red with embarrassment. It was bad enough that Jordan should have kissed her at all, let alone that it had been done in such a public place and witnessed by a chatterbox like Dani. If she should casually mention what she had seen to Russell . . .

'I was just going to drive you all over to Simone's and David's for the day,' Jordan drawled softly.

'That won't be necessary,' Willow refused jerkily, stepping away from the warmth of his arm about her waist.

'Simone's instructions,' he said drily. 'In fact it

was an order; I'm to spend the day with them too.'

Willow frowned her irritation. 'Why didn't you tell me that earlier?' she snapped.

His expression darkened. 'Because I had other things on my mind at the time,' he rasped.

'I'll just bet you did,' she muttered resentfully, then she told Barbara she was going to get their things from their suite. She was sure there would be swimming in the Stewart pool on a lovely day like this, so she was taking their bathing costumes just in case.

'I may as well come with you,' Barbara decided.

'Me too,' said Dani brightly.

'Why don't we all go?' Jordan drawled with obvious sarcasm.

Willow blushed at his derision for her effort to avoid being left alone with him again.

'Dani and I will go,' Barbara told them drily. 'It will be quicker.'

Willow shot her friend a look that clearly said 'traitor!' Barbara was always encouraging her to have more of a social life, to see more of her friends, but especially to allow a man into her life. And heaven knew, enough of them had been after the wealthy divorcee Willow Stewart in the last year! But couldn't Barbara see, despite the kiss she had just witnessed between them, that Jordan was the last man, positively the last man, she should be encouraging? Or the first? Jordan was so strong, a man who knew what he wanted, and allowing nothing and no one to stand in his way of getting it. And she needed someone that strong, to help her to be the same way.

'*Where* do you go when you drift off like that?' Jordan demanded impatiently.

Colour darkened her cheeks once more. 'Aren't a person's thoughts supposed to be their own?' she snapped.

He gave a ragged sigh. 'It's one step forward with you and two steps back, isn't it?'

'Why bother at all, Jordan?' she dismissed wearily. 'And don't say it's because you want me, because that selfish emotion doesn't explain the interest you show in other aspects of my life!'

'I wish——'

'What?' she cut in brittlely. 'That there weren't all these complications attached to wanting your cousin's ex-wife?' she scorned. 'Believe me, I have more complications than any one man could handle.'

'Is Russell included in that?' he rasped.

It *was* Russell. He was where it all ended and began, and no other man could wipe out the memories she had of him.

'What happened between the two of you after you left me last night?' Jordan grasped her arm, his eyes glittering. 'Did he stay with you?'

'No!'

'Did you want him to?'

'Jordan, please!' She tried to pull free of him.

'Did you?' He shook her slightly, his expression intent as he refused to let her break his gaze.

Willow became suddenly still in his arms. 'What do you want me to say?' she challenged heatedly.

'Whatever you want me to say I'll say it.'

'I want the truth?'

'What truth?' she scorned. 'That Russell kissed me and I loved it? That he pulled me down on to the sand and we made love right there and then because we just couldn't wait until we got back to the hotel? Is that the sort of thing you want to hear?' Her eyes glittered with unshed tears as she glared at him defiantly.

'I want the truth, damn it!'

'And don't you think that's it?'

'You—— There, I think that's out.' Jordan's voice changed dramatically from the snarl to smooth lightness in a matter of seconds, releasing her as Barbara and Dani rejoined them, the latter looking at them curiously. 'Willow had some sand in her eye,' he said, explaining away his proximity.

'Yes,' Barbara drawled sceptically, becoming anxious as she looked at Willow's pale face. 'The wind is strong today,' she mocked, stressing the fact that it was a surprisingly still and calm day.

Jordan's mouth tightened. 'Shall we get moving?' he suggested tersely. 'We were expected almost an hour ago.'

Willow wanly returned Barbara's encouraging smiles on the drive over to Simone's and David's. But she couldn't relax. Russell's possessiveness was difficult enough to stand, but having two men jealous over each other was going to be nearly impossible. It would be too much to hope that Russell would behave himself; he never had, so why should he start now?

The Stewart family were already out by the pool when they arrived, the maid arranging for them all to change before joining them there.

'Is everything all right between you and Mr St James?' Barbara prompted softly once Jordan had gone off to another guest bedroom.

'No,' Willow admitted with a pointed look at the listening Dani. 'But I'm sure he'll get over it.'

'He?'

'Yes—he,' she bit out. 'Come on, Dani, let's get changed, shall we? And no talking about what you saw earlier,' she warned teasingly. 'Or Jordan won't give you that lesson on kissing when you're older!' Her daughter's giggles helped to lighten the mood, although she felt herself tense when it came time to go downstairs.

'Ready?' her friend prompted.

Willow took a deep breath. 'As ready as I'll ever be. Try and stick close to me today, hm?'

'We'll do our best,' nodded Barbara.

Doing one's 'best' had never been quite enough when you were up against Russell; he always achieved exactly the result he wanted, and usually without too much effort on his part.

Exactly what result he hoped to achieve today she wasn't sure, but she received a severe jolt when he introduced the raven-haired woman who stood at his side as his girl-friend!

CHAPTER FIVE

THE woman was easily Russell's age, if not older, with long black hair that seemed to curl naturally, a cynicism in her eyes reflected in the twist of her mouth as she smiled. She had a beautiful body, very tall and slender, three tiny triangles of red material saving her modesty. Willow suddenly felt overdressed in her more conservative black bikini!

She looked dazedly from Gemma Laird to Simone and David, trying to gauge their reaction to Russell bringing home a girl-friend, especially a girl-friend like this one. They both returned her look anxiously, seeming as surprised as she was.

Next she looked at Russell, flinching away from the triumph blazing in his eyes, only to find herself looking at Jordan instead. She didn't know of the desperation in her eyes, but she sensed it as Jordan took a protective step towards her, the two of them facing the other couple together now.

'I'm so pleased to meet you.' Gemma Laird held out a languid hand to Willow.

She took it, still dazed. It had never occurred to her that there was another woman in Russell's life! Which was stupid of her when she knew, perhaps better than anyone, what a sensual man he was.

'Russell has spoken of you often.' Gemma Laird

smiled, but it didn't quite reach the hardness of
her eyes.

It was obvious that, whatever Russell had told
the other woman, she didn't like her. The feeling
was definitely mutual.

'Strange,' Jordan was the one to drawl, 'he's
never spoken of you.'

Gemma gave a throaty laugh, looking at him
with appreciation. 'That's probably because it's
natural for the husband to tell the mistress about
his wife, but not so usual the other way around,'
she dismissed. 'I work for Russell. I have done for
some time.'

Did that also mean the two of them had been
having an affair for some time? Willow had a
feeling it did. Strangely she felt nothing at that
realisation, even though she guessed the affair had
probably been going on while she was still married
to Russell. She realised that was what Gemma was
trying to tell her; Willow's only concern was
Russell's ulterior motive in bringing Gemma
Laird here now. Because she knew there had to be
one.

'Daddy?'

Willow gave a pained gasp as she looked down
to find her daughter looking up at Russell with
bewildered eyes. Dani hadn't seen her father for a
year, and it was clear from her expression that she
had expected more of a greeting from him than
being ignored. Not that Russell had ever been too
much of an attentive father, but Dani was
perfectly within her rights to expect more of him

when they hadn't seen each other for such a long time.

'Princess!' drawled Russell, going down on his haunches beside her. 'You haven't grown much!' He ruffled the top of her silky head before straightening again.

Willow had expected no more of him, although she could see Dani was a little hurt. But Russell was the sort of man who should never have had children; he had little time for them and their intrusion into his life, and would probably never have had any of his own if it hadn't influenced Willow into marrying him. But he had been unhappy with that role at best, resenting the time Willow spent with Dani, and from what she could see that certainly hadn't changed.

'She's just petite like her mother.' Jordan swung the little girl up in his arms, making her giggle as he tickled her.

Willow felt grateful for his intervention, having seen Dani's bottom lip start to tremble; she watched as Jordan walked into the pool with her squirming daughter, having turned a moment of awkwardness into a moment of fun. But she was almost afraid to turn and look at Russell, knowing he wouldn't appreciate his cousin's set-down.

The dark anger she saw in his eyes as he watched Jordan and Dani in the pool made her cringe.

'I think your designs are beautiful.' Gemma

Laird diverted her attention, smiling condescendingly. 'I have several of your dresses in my wardrobe.'

'How nice.' Willow's smile lacked its usual warmth as she wondered what position this woman held in Russell's company that she could afford the exclusive creations.

'Russell has such wonderful taste.' Gemma put her arm possessively through the crook of his arm.

Obviously her position in the company didn't call for too much time being spent at the office! 'I——' Willow began.

'Willow, I have a going-home present in the house for Dani,' Simone cut in harshly. 'Could you come and look at it and tell me if you think it's suitable?'

Willow raised dark brows over emerald eyes, sure it was the first time Simone had actively sought her company; wanting her approval on a present for Dani was merely a ruse—Simone had always given Dani exactly what she pleased in the past, and hadn't given a damn if Willow approved or not!

'That dreadful woman,' Simone said agitatedly as she absently got the doll out for Willow to look at. 'I couldn't believe it when Russell walked in with her last night. Or that he would go off to see you the way that he did and just leave us to entertain her. We haven't known what to do with her!'

Willow's mouth twisted. 'Don't tell me you've

met someone more unsuitable for your son than me!'

Blue eyes flashed Simone's anger. 'Don't be flippant, Willow,' she snapped. 'The woman is dreadful, a complete fortune-hunter. My God, she's several years older than Russell!'

Willow shrugged. 'He seems to like her.'

'What man wouldn't?' Simone scorned disparagingly. 'I refuse to believe you designed the dress she almost had on at dinner last night. David couldn't get his gaze above her cleavage!'

Willow doubted Simone saw anything in the least funny about her totally faithful husband ogling a woman's cleavage, so she held back her own smile at David's daring. 'She seems pleasant enough,' she dismissed. 'It's lovely, by the way. I'm sure she'll love it.'

'What—? Oh—oh, you mean the doll,' Simone nodded as if she had never doubted it. 'Actually, I just had to get away for a minute.' She sat down heavily in the bedroom chair.

'I guessed that,' Willow acknowledged drily.

'The strain of trying to entertain that woman is giving me a headache.' Simone shook her head.

'Her name is Gemma,' Willow prompted derisively.

'I know her name,' snapped Simone. 'I don't think I'll ever forgive Russell for bringing her here. My God, what if he actually intends to marry her!' She went pale at the thought.

The idea caused Willow to reflect a little. She didn't think she would be free of Russell even if he did marry again; hadn't he made love to her on the beach last night even though the sensuous Gemma Laird waited at his parents' house for him? But if Russell had the commitment of a wife he certainly wouldn't be able to dictate *her* every move.

'I thought you wanted his happiness, Simone?' She shrugged.

'Yes, but not with a woman like that. God, we've had to put up with one totally unsuitable——' Simone broke off, flushing resentfully as she realised how insulting she had just been. 'We never did get on, Willow,' she bit out. 'And there's no point in being hypocritical about that now, especially as I was proved correct. But I did come to respect you.'

Willow respected the other woman too, knew that everything she did was for what she believed was the good of the family. But as the person who had been on the receiving end of her bitter disapproval, Willow also disliked her intensely. 'Maybe you'll come to respect Gemma Laird, too,' she mocked drily.

'You needn't be so amused at my expense, young lady,' Simone snapped. 'If Russell does marry her she'll be Dani's stepmother! Russell might change his mind about having her for weekends then.'

Willow paled at the thought of Dani spending any length of time alone with Russell, let alone that brittle woman. Russell had been granted visiting rights with Dani at their divorce, and yet they had come to an agreement between them that he would never take Dani away from her overnight. For a price. Except that Russell had never collected on that price. She had to talk to him—alone.

'I care about my own child as much as you care about Danielle,' Simone said heavily. 'And I know he would never be happy with that woman.'

Willow was sceptical about there being a woman alive who Simone *did* believe her son would be happy with, and yet she agreed with her in one respect; Gemma Laird would not be a suitable stepmother for Dani.

Russell, David, and Barbara had taken Jordan's place in the pool with Dani when she emerged back out of the house, the four of them throwing a ball between them. Jordan was now stretched out on a lounger beside an effectively draped Gemma Laird.

'What on earth is she doing now?' gasped Simone as Gemma briefly put her hand on Jordan's thigh as they talked.

'You can't be possessive over your nephew too, Simone,' Willow drawled mockingly, although in truth the casual intimacy of the other woman's caress had given her a nasty jolt too. She hadn't liked seeing Gemma touch Jordan in that way. Which was ridiculous when she had only had dinner with him once. And she hadn't particularly cared when she realised Russell had probably been having an affair with Gemma during their marriage.

Simone shot her an irritated frown. 'Jordan has

more sense than to fall for the wiles of a woman like her.'

'And Russell doesn't?' she taunted.

'For goodness' sake, Willow, forget your differences with me and try to imagine her as Dani's stepmother!'

She already had, and it was totally unacceptable to her. 'Excuse me,' she smiled absently. 'I think I'll join them in the pool.'

'Do that,' Simone snapped impatiently. 'I'd even welcome *you* back into the family if it ever came to a choice between the two of you.'

Willow's mouth twisted. 'I wonder why I don't feel flattered at the admission!'

'How did you expect me to feel about the girl who had tricked my son into marriage?'

'I think you just hit on the answer, Simone,' she said glacially. 'I was a girl, and Russell was a grown man of twenty-eight. Ask yourself which one of us was more likely to be trapped into doing anything.'

'A man can hardly get himself pregnant!' the older woman scorned.

'Exactly,' Willow rasped bitterly, and turned to dive neatly into the pool, the cool water clearing her head. Slowly she swam over to the shallow end of the pool to join the others.

'Thank goodness, the substitute's here,' David said with some relief. 'Barbara and I are losing to Russell and Dani.' He handed her the ball before swimming over to the side and getting out.

It was a boisterous game, and to all intents and

purposes they were a happy family group accompanied by Dani's nanny. But all the adults were aware of the more serious undertones to their relationship.

'Did you and Mother find something nice to talk about?' Russell derided as Barbara and Dani left the pool to get a drink of lemonade.

'Not particularly.' She looked pointedly to where Gemma Laird was all but draping herself over Jordan.

Russell followed her gaze. 'Sometimes Mother can be so unsubtle,' he drawled.

'Not only your mother!'

He shrugged. 'Look on the bright side, Willow; even you look good as a daughter-in-law to her now!'

She sighed. 'Russell, what is that woman doing here?'

'"That woman" happens to be my guest,' he rasped, 'and should be treated as such!'

'I haven't been impolite to her,' she denied, shaking her head.

'None of you have, but you haven't exactly been *polite* either. Except Jordan.' He watched his cousin with narrowed eyes as he still chatted amiably with Gemma Laird. 'Obviously Jordan isn't so jaded he can't still appreciate a beautiful woman.'

'Why should he be?' Willow snapped. 'He isn't that old.'

Russell's gaze levelled on her speculatively. 'You always used to think so.'

Her cheeks were suddenly flushed. 'Only because I was so young.'

'Hm,' he murmured mockingly. 'And now you feel old, is that it?'

'Ancient!' she confirmed bitterly.

'Well, it makes little difference, because my surprise at him flirting with first you and now Gemma has nothing to do with Jordan's age.'

Willow looked at him sharply, a little warily. 'What do you mean?'

'You're very interested in my cousin all of a sudden,' Russell taunted.

Her blush deepened. 'Not really, it's just that you're making all this sound so mysterious.'

He grinned his satisfaction at unnerving her so that her voice was raised in anger. 'It's a deep, dark family secret, that's why.'

'What is?' she said irritably.

'I said it's a family secret, Willow,' he drawled.

She drew in an angry breath. 'And I'm no longer a member of that élite bunch!' She turned away in anger, furious with herself as much as with Russell for letting him draw her in this way.

'Hey,' he chided, grabbing her arm, 'I was only teasing you!' He looked at her with mocking eyes.

'You don't know how to tease, Russell,' she sighed. 'Now let me go.'

'Please,' he prompted hardly, his fingers tightening slightly.

'Please!' she rasped.

'Don't you want to know Jordan's secret?' he taunted as she turned away the moment she was released.

She did, he knew she did!

'It seems,' he said slowly, 'that accidents in family planning run in the family!'

The colour drained from her face, leaving her ghostly white. 'You mean Jordan . . .' she muttered in sudden realisation.

Russell nodded, his expression one of satisfaction. 'It wasn't quite the same, of course,' he drawled. 'Claudia was older than Jordan, and it wasn't love between them either. But accidents will happen in even the most basic of relationships.'

'What happened to—to Claudia? And the baby?' Her eyes were wide with bewilderment. There had never been any mention of Jordan having a wife . . .

Russell shrugged. 'As I said, the relationship was an affair at best, not even that on Jordan's part, and so he hesitated about committing himself to a marriage with a woman he didn't love. What's the saying, "he who hesitates, loses"? It's close enough, anyway,' he dismissed. 'While Jordan was hesitating, and making plans to take care of the baby himself once it was born, Claudia met someone else who was just as wealthy, but he didn't want to marry her when she was expecting some other man's baby, even if the father would have taken it once it was born.'

Harlequin's

Best-Ever
"Get Acquainted"
Offer

Look what we'd give to hear from you

▲ **GET ALL YOU ARE
ENTITLED TO—AFFIX STICKER
TO RETURN CARD—MAIL TODAY** ▲

This is our most fabulous offer ever...
AND THERE'S STILL MORE INSIDE.

Let's get acquainted.
Let's become friends—

Look what we've got for you:

5 FREE GIFT

…A FREE compact Harlequin umbrella …plus a sampler set of 4 terrific Harlequin Presents novels, specially selected by our editors.

FREE MYSTERY GIFT

…PLUS a surprise mystery gift that will delight you.

All this just for trying our Reader Service!

With your trial, you'll get SNEAK PREVIEWS to 8 new Harlequin Presents novels a month— before they're available in stores—with 10% off retail on any books you keep (just $2.24 each)— plus 89¢ postage and handling per shipment.

Plus There's More!

You'll also get our newsletter, packed with news of your favorite authors and upcoming books—FREE! And as a valued reader, we'll be sending you additional free gifts from time to time—as a token of our appreciation.

THERE IS NO CATCH. You're not required to buy a single book, ever. You may cancel Reader Service privileges anytime, if you want. The free gifts are yours anyway. It's a super sweet deal if ever there was one. Try us and see!

Get 4 FREE full-length Harlequin Presents novels.

Plus

this handy compact umbrella

Plus

a surprise free gift

▼ PLUS LOTS MORE! MAIL THIS CARD TODAY ▼

Don't forget...

...Return this card today to receive your 4 free books, free compact umbrella and free mystery gift.

...You will receive books before they're available in stores and at a discount off retail prices.

...No obligation. Keep only the books you want, cancel anytime.

If offer card is missing, write to: Harlequin Reader Service, P.O. Box 609, Fort Erie, Ontario, L2A 5X3.

'You mean Claudia—she——'
'Aborted the baby and married the other man.'
Russell nodded callously.

CHAPTER SIX

'ANOTHER drink?'

Willow raised startled lids to look at Jordan, giving an abrupt smile as she shook her head in refusal, listening abstractedly as he requested another drink for himself from the hovering waiter, while soft piano music was being played in the lounge just off the bar where they sat.

She had been taken aback when Jordan had arrived at the hotel after dinner, feeling uncomfortable with him after what Russell had told her about him this afternoon. She didn't doubt Russell was telling the truth; he had never needed to lie to be able to hurt her. And she was hurt, now knowing the reason Jordan had always held her in so much contempt, why he had made it clear that he could now only desire her, believing that *she* had actually got the man she had set out to entrap. There could be no doubt that was what he believed; his remarks when she arrived three days ago had been blunt and to the point.

'You're very quiet,' he prompted now. 'Thinking of the work you have to do when you get back?'

She hadn't given the fashion show a second thought, and her surprised expression must have shown that.

Jordan chuckled. 'No, I don't think so. Is it

Gemma?' he probed, his gaze intent.

The picture of the other woman as her hand trailed along the nakedness of Jordan's thigh instantly came to mind, and anger flared in her eyes. 'I think she's what's known as a "man's woman",' she scorned.

He gave an inclination of his head. 'She is a little overwhelming.'

'You should know!' Contrition washed over her as she realised how bitchy she sounded. 'I'm sorry,' she sighed. 'It's just that this visit has been even more traumatic than I thought it would be.' Because Russell had chosen to come here at the same time!

Jordan's mouth firmed; he looked very dark and attractive in the black evening suit and snowy white shirt. 'It seemed to be going fine until Russell arrived,' he gratingly echoed her thoughts.

She gave him a mocking look. 'You mean your seduction was working?'

He frowned darkly. 'I wasn't seducing you, Willow; we were enjoying each other.'

Yes, she had enjoyed her time in this man's arms, and feeling as she did about Russell that knowledge still surprised her. And knowing how Russell felt about her she knew he must never know the full extent of her response to Jordan.

'Willow, I want you to come home with me tonight——'

'No!' she gasped, looking about them uncomfortably as several of the other people in the bar turned to look at them as her vehement refusal carried beyond their table. 'No,' she repeated huskily.

Jordan's hand captured hers in a firm grasp. 'I need you. And I think you need me.'

'What do you need me for, Jordan?' she scorned, believing she already knew the answer to that.

'To hold. To caress.' His compelling gaze refused to release hers, his eyes like dark velvet. 'It's something we all need at times. Even me,' he added with self-derision.

'And do I look in need of—being held?' she mocked, all the time her heart beating wildly, her hand cold in his, despite the warmth of the evening.

'Yes.'

Willow drew in a ragged breath at the bluntness of his answer, wishing there *were* someone to just hold her and tell her everything was going to be all right. But it wasn't, and it never would be.

Her head went back challengingly. 'You're wrong, Jordan. I don't need anyone but my daughter.'

'Dani is a child, and it isn't a child's love you need,' he rasped.

If Russell hadn't told her what he had about Jordan earlier she might have been tempted to seek comfort in the arms of the man she already knew could make her forget everything else but him. But in Jordan's mind it was only the fact that she decided to have her child that made her any different from the treacherous Claudia from his own past. She had gone to one man's bed for all the wrong reasons; she couldn't go to Jordan for different but just as wrong reasons.

'You're forgetting Russell,' she taunted. 'He's always been only too happy to give me all the loving attention I need.'

'Aren't *you* forgetting the existence of Gemma Laird?' Jordan rasped.

'I don't think so,' she said with a dismissive shake of her head. 'Miss Laird made no secret of the fact their affair has been going on for some years, and I can assure you Russell was never reluctant to share my bed in the past.'

His mouth tightened. 'You and Russell aren't good for each other,' he bit out. 'You've changed since he arrived, and I don't think I've ever seen him this strung out.' He frowned.

'Jordan,' she sighed. 'Russell, and consequently our relationship, are none of your business.'

'I want to be your friend——'

'The very intimate kind!' she derided.

He frowned, brown velvet eyes levelled on her censoriously. 'Maybe we should postpone this conversation until you're back in London.'

When Russell had made it perfectly clear he intended being back in her life, her year of 'freedom' being over as far as he was concerned. 'No,' she snapped, standing up. 'Look, if you'll excuse me, I have to go and help Barbara finish packing; we leave very early in the morning.'

'Willow, don't push me away.' Jordan had risen too and was standing very close to her. I—would it make a difference if I told you I was coming to care for you?' He looked at her almost resentfully.

Willow was perfectly aware that the admission had been forced out of him, and she searched his face wonderingly. He couldn't actually be serious, not after what Russell had told her about Claudia. And yet, like Russell, she doubted he was a man who said what he didn't mean. It was a complication, in the light of Russell's declaration last night, that she didn't need. And yet how good it would feel to lose herself in Jordan's velvet touch, to just feel herself cosseted and cared for, for once, instead of being the one who always had to be strong.

She swallowed hard. 'I'm sorry, Jordan.' She shook her head, genuinely regretful.

Fire blazed in his eyes. 'What more do you want from me?'

'Peace,' she sighed. 'It seems to be an expensive commodity.' She walked away, a splash of exotic colour in the red and black dress capped by her silver-blonde hair. She had never felt so lonely, and alone, in her life.

'I think you're a fool,' Barbara admonished when she had been told of Jordan's invitation as the two of them quickly completed the packing. 'He's a good man, I'm sure of it.'

'He's also Russell's cousin.'

'And their characters are as different as chalk and cheese!'

'I don't want to get involved, with any man,' Willow maintained doggedly.

'One failed marriage doesn't have to sour you off all men,' her friend cautioned.

'Jordan has already been hurt enough.' She shook her head.

Barbara watched her closely. 'So you refused for his sake?'

'How do you think he would feel if he knew the whole truth about me?' she sighed wearily.

'Outraged, I should think,' Barbara said disgustedly. 'You certainly didn't try to trap anyone into marriage. And maybe he realises that.'

'Does he?' Willow said heavily, plucking absently at the brocade on the arm of the chair she now sat in.

Her friend sighed her impatience. 'Why don't you just give the man a chance?'

'I can't.'

'Russell?'

She chewed on her inner lip. 'He warned me to stay away from Jordan.'

'So that's why you were so reluctant to join Mr St James tonight,' Barbara realised indignantly. 'Willow, you can't live the rest of your life under the dictates of that man!'

'I can't *not*,' she corrected heavily. 'We both know that.'

'Russell Stewart is a tyrant and a——'

'Let's order ourselves some coffee,' she cut in decisively. 'Thank goodness we can leave here early tomorrow!'

Although that knowledge gave her little real comfort, knowing Russell meant what he said

about her freedom being over. But how far did he
mean his hold on her to go this time? That was the
question that plagued her so that she didn't feel in
the least like going to bed, although her sketch pad
remained untouched on her knee as she stared off
into space.

She and Barbara both made a grab for the
telephone before its ringing woke Dani when it
rang shortly after half past ten, and Willow smiled
at Barbara as she was the one to answer the call,
her smile fading as the caller identified himself.

'I'm downstairs in the bar,' Russell bit out. 'I
want to talk to you.'

Her hand tightened about the receiver. 'Why
don't you come up here instead?' she invited
breathlessly, not liking the sound of his voice at
all. He wasn't usually a man who resorted to
alcohol to bolster his mood, but tonight he
definitely sounded as if he had been drinking, and
she didn't want him to have access to more.

'Because the conscientious Miss Gibbons would
be an interested party to our conversation that I
dont need,' he scorned.

'But——'

'Don't make me come and get you, Willow,' he
rasped coldly. 'Get yourself down here!'

The crash as he slammed down the receiver
reverberated around the room and Willow was
very pale as she looked up at Barbara.

'You don't have to go,' her friend told her
grimly.

'Oh yes.' There was a slight catch in her throat.

'I do.' She picked up her cashmere wrap, suddenly cold. 'Wish me luck, Barbara; I have a feeling this is going to be it!'

Barbara looked furious. 'He can't force you to do anything.'

Willow gave a bitter smile. 'No?' she sneered before leaving the suite to join Russell in the bar, both women knowing it was the last thing she wanted to be doing.

He sat on one of the high stools that fronted the bar, getting down to sit at one of the more private tables when she joined him. By the flush to his cheeks and the reckless glitter in his eyes she knew her initial instinct had been correct; he had been drinking. Or something equally destructive. He had never used drugs that she knew of during their marriage, but there was a first time for everything. For Russell.

'You look lovely—as usual,' he drawled in a derisive voice.

'Thank you,' she accepted coolly.

'Drink?'

'No, thank you.' She sat tensely on the edge of her seat, wanting to dispel the impression of nervousness she knew she must be giving. 'No Gemma Laird tonight?' She raised mocking brows.

His mouth twisted. 'What would you say if I told you she's with Jordan?' he taunted.

Willow's mind went a complete blank at this unexpected answer. Jordan with Gemma? And then she remembered his mood when he had left

her almost two hours ago; he certainly hadn't been
in the mood to go to Gemma Laird!

'I wouldn't believe it,' she dismissed
confidently.

'Of him?' Russell rasped. 'Or of her?'

She believed Gemma Laird was capable of
doing anything to get what she wanted, including
seducing another man into her bed while conduct-
ing a long-standing affair. 'I would say you know
her much better than I do.' She shrugged.

'As you know Jordan better than I do?' His
voice was dangerously soft.

Her heart lurched at the trap he had set for her.
'I've already told you, I don't know Jordan at all.'

'I hope not, for your sake,' he muttered grimly.

'And what does that mean?' she bristled warily.

'It means I've decided we should finish our
conversation of the other night after all,' he told
her with satisfaction.

Willow moistened her suddenly dry lips with the
tip of her tongue. 'What conversation was that?'
But she knew, she *knew*.

Russell's mouth twisted at her evasiveness. 'The
one about our plans when we get back to London,'
he said, mocking her convenient lapse of memory.

'Oh, that one.' She attempted lightness, knowing she failed miserably. But she didn't want to
hear this!

Russell's thumb moved rhythmically against the
back of her hand. 'Would you like to hear them?'

She swallowed hard. 'Yes.'

'I've decided that we're going to remarry.' He

watched her like a cat with a cornered mouse.

'No!' She choked refusal, her hands clenching on the edge of the table.

Mocking blue eyes gleamed his satisfaction. 'Oh yes,' he confirmed softly, his gaze snapping angrily at the pallor of her cheeks. 'For God's sake, Willow, you know I love you——'

'I know you have a very strange way of showing love,' she accused, her breathing ragged. She couldn't become this man's wife again, she just couldn't!

'You've never allowed me to show my love the way that I wanted to,' he snapped. 'You never wanted it.'

'And you know why!'

He gave an impatient sigh. 'Get used to the idea, Willow, because you will be marrying me again. It wasn't a proposal, it was an order!'

'And if I refuse to do it?'

'Then all past deals and agreements are off.' He stood up. 'I hope I've made myself clear?' He looked down at her with frosty eyes.

She swallowed hard. 'Very clear.'

'Your answer?' he grated.

'When do you want the remarriage to take place?' she asked shakily.

His head went back arrogantly, as if her acceptance had never been in doubt. As it hadn't! 'As soon as I can arrange it!'

Willow numbly ordered herself a brandy once he had left, signed for it, drank half of it before she was able to stop trembling. She felt so alone, so utterly helpless——

Jordan. Jordan always stopped her feeling that way, he would hold her until the worst of the pain went away. And if he demanded her body in payment of that comfort, then so be it; it couldn't be any worse than what Russell was demanding she do.

CHAPTER SEVEN

JORDAN looked very big and dark with the golden glow of the illuminated hallway behind him, still wearing the black trousers to his evening suit, his jacket discarded, his shirt unbuttoned at the throat. His face was partially in shadow too, while Willow was clearly illuminated as she stood outside his front door, hoping she didn't look as vulnerable as she felt.

This had been a bad idea, she realised now that she was no longer blinded by the need to be held in his arms and told everything was going to be all right even when she knew it wasn't. She had just been tempted by the comfort he seemed to offer. But it would serve no purpose; Russell would still be there, and coming here would probably just make Jordan despise her more than he already did.

'Come in,' he invited gruffly as he seemed to sense her decision.

'I—er—I don't think I'll bother, after all.' She shook her head, her movements nervy. 'I shouldn't have come here.'

'Why did you?' he probed gently.

It was that very gentleness that was her undoing. 'I don't know——' she managed to choke before her face crumpled and she began to sob.

She was vaguely aware of being drawn into the strength of Jordan's arms, of being guided inside the house, the door closing behind them as she was enveloped in a comforting warmth.

When the tears at last began to subside she was seated on the sofa, held gently but firmly against Jordan's chest. And she had no idea what to do next, she couldn't tell Jordan why she was so upset. He offered comfort, but not that much comfort!

'Does Barbara know where you are?' he asked softly as he stroked her hair.

She silently shook her head, guilt washing over her as she realised she had walked out of the hotel without a thought for the fact that Barbara would be worrying about her, or that Dani could have woken up and needed her.

Jordan went to stand up, hesitating. 'You aren't hurt? No one—touched you?'

'No.' Her eyes were wide with shock as she looked at him. It hadn't occurred to her that he would think something like that!

He nodded abruptly. 'Then I'll just call Barbara and tell her you're with me. and that you're staying the night——'

'Oh, I can't do that.' She shook her head.

His expression was grim. 'Willow, allow me to be the judge of what you can and cannot do,' he bit out. 'And you're in no fit state to go anywhere else tonight.'

Her weeping had exhausted her, if the truth were known, and she sat weakly back in the chair as she listened to Jordan's end of the conversation as he talked to Barbara. The conversation was short, with Barbara seeming to ask few questions, Jordan's replies being brief and to the point.

'Shower, and then bed for you, young lady,' he told her firmly seconds later. 'And don't worry,' he teased, 'I have several guest bedrooms; you can take your pick of them!'

Willow smiled her gratitude at this thoughtfulness, having taken the comfort and strength of his embrace, but knowing the physical payment for that strength was beyond her at the moment. She hesitated. 'You're sure I'm not being a bother to you?'

'I'm glad you came to me.' His gaze was darkly intent. 'Now, how do you like your shower water, hot, warm, or cool?' He briskly changed the subject, pulling her to her feet.

'Hot, please,' she said gratefully.

The bedroom Jordan escorted her to obviously wasn't his own, with its bright lemon and cream décor, the adjoining bathroom fitted out with similar colours, only the addition of the thick brown bath towels being different.

Jordan sat her down on the side of the bed while he went to judge the temperature of the water.

'Perfect,' he said with satisfaction, and came over to her to begin unbuttoning the front of her dress.

'Calm down,' he drawled as she raised startled eyes to his. 'I've seen you naked before—or almost,' he amended softly. 'And you're too exhausted to do it for yourself.'

She did feel very weak, and it did feel so nice to have someone else take charge of her. Jordan was not imposing his much stronger will on her as he could have done, merely caring for her. She didn't even feel any awkwardness when the removal of her dress revealed only a pair of lacy briefs. Jordan quickly dispensed with them too, before gently urging her beneath the water.

There was something so soothing about standing under the pounding spray of a shower, thought becoming unnecessary while she was just enjoying the feel of the water on her body.

'Don't go and fall asleep in there.' Jordan tapped lightly on the door when she had been in the shower for several minutes.

The shower had refreshed her; she felt—now what was it Jordan had once described her as?— new and untouched. She wanted to be untouched for him tonight. 'Why don't you join me?' she invited huskily.

'What?'

She swallowed hard. 'I said, why don't you join me?' She made her voice louder this time. The silence that greeted her invitation on the other side of the door made her nervous.

Suddenly the door swung open and a completely naked Jordan stepped inside the shower with her. 'I thought you'd never ask!' His gaze never wavered from hers as he took the soap from her suddenly still hands and began to wash her. 'It's been pure purgatory standing on the other side of this glass door being able to see the outline of your body but unable to touch!'

He was magnificent to look at. She had seen him in bathing trunks dozens of times and had always known how beautifully muscular he was. But without that small article of clothing he was even more so, so blatantly male, the maleness hard and throbbing as his hands moved over her body.

'Aren't you curious to know what I was upset about earlier?' Her voice was husky, her body burning where he touched, her legs trembling as he touched between her thighs.

'Naturally I am.'

'Well?' she prompted impatiently as he said nothing else.

'Saying no to me?' he mocked.

'No.' She smiled at his levity about something that had so angered him earlier.

'Willow, do you want to tell me about it?' he probed softly.

She gave a ragged sigh. 'No.'

'Do you want *me*?'

'I—I think so.' She couldn't quite meet his gaze, her poise shattered by the bluntness of his query.

'Willow,' he tilted her chin, looking straight into her eyes. 'This— being together this way, it doesn't have to lead to anything else,' he assured her. 'I'm just enjoying touching you.'

'Is it enough?' she frowned.

'It is if you say it is,' he nodded.

She swallowed hard. 'I don't want you to think I'm playing games with you.'

'I know you aren't,' he dismissed, stroking her cheek.

'Russell told me what Claudia did to you——' She broke off as his expression darkened. 'He only did it to show me why you've despised me all these years,' she explained hastily.

'I don't despise you.' Jordan shook his head. 'Willow, Claudia was a long time ago——'

'But what she did to you did influence how you felt about me.'

'Did,' he acknowledged harshly. 'But these last few days I've come to realise you're nothing like her. The fact that you had your baby should have told me that; there are ways of ridding yourself of a baby you don't want even after the father has married you. And the mercenary I always believed you were would never have taken care of Dani as a baby, exclusively, the way that you did.'

'I always wanted Dani,' she choked.

Jordan nodded. 'And some day I want you to tell me all about your marriage to Russell. But not tonight,' he decided briskly. 'I don't think you can take any more tonight.'

'I—I think I'd like you to make love to me now, Jordan.' She looked at him shyly.

Pleasure flooded the darkness of his eyes, only to be quickly brought under control again. 'You're under no obligation . . .'

'I *want* you,' she said exasperatedly.

He smiled at her aggression. 'There's no need to get angry about it!'

This indulgent teasing had never been a part of

her marriage to Russell, and she reacted to it like a
child to the beauty of a flower or the softness of a
kitten, blossoming in front of his eyes as she shyly
raised her mouth to capture his.

'My turn.' His voice was husky as he raised his
head to hand her the soap, his eyes very dark.

'Velvet,' Willow murmured wonderingly.

'You haven't touched me yet,' he mocked.

'I meant your eyes,' she chided reprovingly,
blushing profusely.

'Oh, those.' He nodded teasingly.

How could she have ever thought the man was
cold and arrogant! He was the most wonderful
man she had ever met; kind, understanding and,
most of all, gentle.

He stood completely still as she used the soap to
wash him slowly all over, trembling a little as she
caressed the shuddering hardness of his desire,
finally pulling her up against him with a groan.

'Let's go to bed, Willow,' he urged shakily.

For all his urgency he took the time to dry her
body, slowly from top to toe, although he didn't
have the control to wait while she did the same
thing to him, towelling himself with the minimum
amount of time for his body to no longer glisten
with droplets of water, his face nuzzling against
her throat as they walked through to the bedroom.

But as they lay down together Willow experienced a nervousness she had never known before, feeling as if this were the very first time a
man had made love to her. She had thought it

wouldn't matter that Jordan would be disappointed in her as a bed partner, but now she realised it
did matter; she wanted him to find pleasure in her
arms. But she didn't know how to give it to him,
not in the way she wanted to.

Jordan felt her trembling against him. 'Relax,
Willow,' he soothed. 'It doesn't have to be now, we
have all night.'

Waiting would change nothing, she knew that
now, and what pleasure she had known in his arms
quickly faded as her thoughts dwelled on what he
was going to do to her. She had been a fool to think
she could feel any differently with Jordan!

'Willow?' he prompted as he frowned down at
her. 'Darling, what is it?'

Darling; it was a word for lovers. 'I don't love
you, Jordan,' she told him flatly.

'I know that,' he acknowledged softly. 'But you
do need me.'

She didn't think he had believed she loved him,
and yet even so she was disappointed in his easy
acceptance of her denial. 'I thought I did——'

'It's all right, Willow,' he soothed. 'I told you,
nothing has to happen. We'll just go to sleep
together holding each other like this.' He rested
her head down on his shoulder, his arms about her.

She looked up at him uncertainly. Could he just
do that, turn off when seconds ago his body had
been straining against hers in complete arousal?
Russell never had, but perhaps Jordan—— No, he
couldn't either, and his arousal reacted strongly as
she moved her hand lightly across his thighs. But

he was able to control it, and his eyes closed as he attempted to go to sleep.

The tears fell softly against her cheeks.

Jordan turned slightly as he felt her quiver, brown eyes searching in the darkness. 'please don't cry again,' he groaned. 'I can't bear it if you do!'

But she couldn't stop, burying her face against his chest, her tears wetting his hard flesh.

'Willow, no! Please, darling.' He rained kisses on her brow, her eyes, across her cheeks. 'Please, Willow,' he choked, before his mouth hotly claimed hers.

The only oblivion was his mouth on hers, and she returned his kiss with heated passion, arching up into him as she sought his desire, tasting him, drawing his tongue into her mouth as it sought entrance, thrusting into her gently.

One of his hands, those beautiful hands, trailed up her body to cup her breast, and tremors racked her body as he lightly caressed the aching tip. After Dani was born she hadn't been able to bear Russell's touch on her breasts, but once again her reaction to Jordan's caress shook her off balance, and a fire burned between her thighs as he lowered his head to capture the other nipple in his mouth.

His back felt hard with muscle, and yet his skin was as soft as silk as she clung to him, the fire in her body becoming a flame as she felt him moving even lower down her body. 'No— Please——' She broke off with a groan as a sensation unlike any other she had ever known spiralled through her body, until it seemed that every inch of her were about to explode.

'Guide me into you, Willow,' he urged raggedly. 'I don't want to hurt you.'

She felt her own moistness as she took him in her hand and guided him slowly inside her. 'Velvet,' she murmured again, feeling the hard strength of him inside her as he began to move against her.

'Yes.' He groaned agreement of the sensations he was experiencing, controlling the depth and the force of his thrusts, his mouth moistly open on hers.

She didn't know what was happening to her, her hips raised to meet the thrust of his as she matched his rhythm, knowing the moment he lost control and began to thrust into her without conscious thought, convulsively driven on to bring them both to that moment of complete pleasure. Willow felt a heat engulf her body, flaming out of contol as spasms began to course through her, gasping as she felt them build into a crescendo, the fiery ache of release shaking her whole body at the same moment as Jordan arched into her, flooding her with his passion.

Her body still glowed with that elating pleasure even after the fierce intensity of the heat had become a throbbing ache. She clung to Jordan's shoulder, wanting him to stay inside her for ever.

'Thank you,' Jordan murmured against her throat, their bodies glistening with perspiration.

'Thank *me*?' she asked, feeling as if she should

get down on her knees and and thank *him* for the wonderful gift he had just given her.

He looked down at her with sensuously sleepy brown eyes, a dark lock of hair falling endearingly across his forehead. 'I wanted you so much,' he admitted gruffly. 'You were so much more than I dared hope for.'

She swallowed hard. 'I was?'

He drew in a ragged breath, leaning on his elbows to look down at her flushed face. 'I completely lost control,' he said ruefully.

'Doesn't that—normally happen, when you make love?' Willow blinked up at him.

His mouth twisted. 'Not for several years, no,' he admitted drily.

'Not since—Claudia?' she probed hesitantly, wondering if he had loved the other woman after all.

Jordan's eyes narrowed. 'Not because I loved her,' he instantly disputed that belief, 'but because she showed me what bitches women can be. When did Russell tell you about her?'

'This afternoon.' Her voice was husky, their bodies still intimately joined. This was something else that was new to her; she and Russell had always moved instantly apart after they had made love.

'Why?' Jordan frowned.

'Why?' she repeated, raising startled lids, looking shyly into the face of the man who was her lover, whose body was still merged with her own. 'So that this shouldn't happen, I suppose.'

'He does still want you himself,' Jordan realised grimly. 'And you?' he probed harshly.

'You can ask me *that*? Now?' Her voice was pained.

His expression gentled at the hurt in her eyes. 'I'm sorry.'

'Are you?' Her only defence was anger. 'Next you'll be asking me which of you I think is the better lover!'

His eyes glittered dangerously before he quickly masked his emotions. 'I would never ask any woman that!' he bit out coldly.

Her pride was grateful for that, because the answer was too humiliating. 'I thought perhaps with the rivalry that has always existed between the two of you——'

'There is no rivalry,' rasped Jordan. 'Except, perhaps, in Russell's mind. And I'd really rather not discuss your ex-husband at the moment!' He bent his head to roughly claim her mouth.

Willow had believed she had incited violence in him, and while it was an emotion she feared, it was one she understood. But although Jordan's love-making was fierce it was underlined with tenderness, and her senses received another surprise as she felt herself respond to his ferocity with a little fierceness of her own, her nails digging into his back as her legs wrapped themselves about him, her climax more intense this time than the last.

'God, I'm sorry.' His body still trembled inside hers as he buried his face in her throat. 'I didn't mean to lose my temper.'

'I did, with you,' she admitted ruefully. 'I was hurt—about what you had said.'

Jordan sighed raggedly. 'That was no excuse for what I just did.'

She frowned. 'What did you just do?'

'Made love to you in anger,' he said self-disgustedly.

Oh no, she was an expert on what it was like to be made love to in anger, and that hadn't been it. Jordan might have been furious with her, but nothing could erase the tenderness that was such a fundamental part of him, and so much in evidence when he made love to her.

'Jordan.' She smoothed the hair at his brow, wanting so much to remain with him this way and yet knowing they only had tonight. 'We have a few more hours left until morning . . .'

Desire flared in his eyes. 'It isn't true what women say about men being sexual athletes, you know,' he drawled.

'No?' she mocked, feeling the desire throb back into his body. 'Not all men, perhaps,' she acknowledged throatily. 'Then I must be one of the lucky women that found one!'

He laughed huskily. 'Would you believe me if I told you this never happened to me before?'

'What hasn't?'

'Neither the intensity, or the way I instantly want you again.'

Willow looked up into the warm sincerity of his eyes, drowning in their softness. 'Yes.'

'This has *never* happened to me before!' he

growled, before the fiery lovemaking controlled them once again.

Willow was bleary-eyed from lack of sleep as she sat across the breakfast table from Jordan at six o'clock the next morning as he fed her with scrambled eggs, toast, and very strong coffee. They both needed the latter after the little sleep they had had during the last few hours.

She was a little shy with him after the night of lovemaking that had just passed between them. She hadn't dreamt there was such sensual pleasure as Jordan had shown her, not just once, or twice, but several times. She had never experienced anything like that with Russell, and she was glad Jordan had been the one to show her that paradise. Even if it could only be for one night . . .

But she wouldn't think of it ending yet; she still had a few minutes with him before she had to join Barbara and Dani at the hotel where they were getting ready to catch the early flight to London, even as she gazed dreamily at Jordan.

'This may sound hackneyed . . .' his voice was huskily soft, 'but last night was beautiful.'

'Yes.'

'It's never been like that for me before,' he added throatily, his eyes velvety soft. 'So natural, so—so damned incredible!'

'No.'

'For you either?'

'No,' she answered truthfully. Surely that perfection only happened once in a lifetime?

Jordan sighed. 'I realise now isn't the time, but we really have to talk about Rus——'

'As you said, now isn't the time.' Her gaze was suddenly evasive, her mood of contentment shattered.

'I'm sorry.' His hand grasped hers across the table. 'It can wait,' he dismissed. 'It will all have to wait until I join you in London for the weekend. Tomorrow night. I really do have to put in an appearance at my office during the day.'

'Last night was——' Willow moistened her lips. 'It was very good. But it can't happen again.' She shook her head decisively.

'I understand it could be awkward for Dani,' he nodded. 'But she accepts me as her uncle, and we can be discreet when we're both with her.'

'It isn't a question of that——'

'Willow, I understand the fashion show means a lot to you——'

'It isn't even that,' she dismissed gruffly, not having given the show a second thought in the last few hours. 'Jordan, last night was it.'

'It?' he echoed slowly, his body tense.

'The beginning and end of our affair,' she explained quickly. 'There can't be any more.'

'Why the hell not?' he rasped, once again the Jordon St James she had always known, arrogance etched into his rugged features. 'I don't just want a one-night stand!'

Neither did she. Last night, with Jordan, she had discovered all the joys of being a woman. She hungered to know that joy again and again with

him, and she didn't give him up lightly. 'It was
hardly as cheap and nasty as that, Jordan,' she
dismissed in a controlled voice. 'It was a beautiful
night of love between two people who wanted each
other.'

'Then why does it have to end if it was so good?'
His eyes were narrowed. 'I still want you. And I
know you still want me.'

That couldn't be doubted when she quivered
with desire each time he so much as touched her!
'We lead different lives, Jordan——'

'We lead lives that could be ideal for us seeing
each other—both of us are pretty caught up in our
careers during the week, and the weekend could be
for us to be together.'

'I spend my weekends with Dani; it's a special
time for us.'

'I'm sure she isn't going to mind if I join you,' he
rasped.

'*I'll* mind,' she told him heatedly. 'Jordan, what
does it take to say no to you?'

'The truth.' He watched with narrowed eyes as
she stiffened tensely. 'I didn't ask last night, but
I'm asking now.'

Willow moistened her lips. 'What?'

'What *did* happen to upset you last night?'

Her shrug was deliberately casual. 'It's not
important any more.'

'It was important enough to you last night to
make you come to me!'

'Was it?' she dismissed with deliberation. 'It's
always so—difficult, for a woman to change her

mind without appearing like——' She watched him surreptitiously, willing him to believe that was all that had happened.

Jordan drew in a ragged breath. 'Are you telling me that was what happened last night?'

'I'm telling you I changed my mind about wanting you, yes.' She nodded abruptly.

He looked at her searchingly for several minutes before standing up. 'Why not, it's a woman's prerogative, after all,' he drawled, pulling back her chair for her.

Willow eyed him warily, but found only bland acceptance of her explanation in his expression. She trusted that blandness about as much as she trusted Russell—which was not at all! 'Jordan——'

'You'll have to leave now if you're to catch your plane,' he reminded her lightly.

'But——' She broke off as he pulled her towards the door. 'Jordan, don't take it into your head to pay me any surprise visits in the near future, because——'

'I wouldn't presume to intrude in that way. Besides,' he added with a frown, 'a gentleman should never try to force a woman into changing her mind once she's come to a decision.'

On the way back to the hotel her disquiet increased; it continued on the flight back to London, and even when she and Dani went out shopping for food later that morning she still felt uneasy. In the end Jordan had accepted too easily that she didn't want to see him again; he had been too amiable. She had a feeling, despite all her protestations to the contrary, that she was going to see Jordan again very soon. She dreaded to think what Russell's reaction to his cousin calling on her in London would be!

She didn't expect to see Jordan quite as soon as she did though!

'All right, all right,' she muttered as she hurried to answer the door, tying the belt to her robe as she did so. People shouldn't come calling at eleven o'clock at night in the first place!

If Jordan had looked amiable and relaxed the last time she had seen him, he now looked the opposite, his dark suit creased, his hair falling over his forehead, his expression one of furious impatience.

'Jordan . . .' She leant weakly against the door. 'I thought we had agreed——'

'That was before.' He pushed his way inside, his eyes narrowing angrily on Barbara as she came sleepily into the lounge, all of them having decided on an early night after the long day they had all had. With a self-conscious 'Excuse me', Barbara hastily left the room again.

Willow agitatedly followed Jordan into the lounge, feeling very young and vulnerable with her hair mussed and her face bare of make-up. 'Before what?' she prompted irritably.

Jordan faced her with steady eyes, his mouth a furious slash above his clenched jaw. 'Last night I didn't push you for answers. This morning I asked for them, but now I'm *demanding* them!' he thundered.

She clenched her hands together in front of her. 'I gave you the answer——'

'You gave me *an* answer,' he grated. 'Not the right one, unfortunately.'

'Jordan——'

'Thanks for the invitation, by the way. Although I would rather have received it personally,' he added grimly, a nerve pulsing in his jaw.

She shook her head. 'I didn't invite you here. I told you——'

'Not that invitation,' he rasped impatiently. 'Although Russell's invitation does give me a more in-depth answer as to why you decided last night was enough between us.'

Willow felt as if all the breath had been knocked from her body. 'Russell's invitation?'

'Don't look so upset because your secret is out,' Jordan jeered. 'Russell naturally wanted to invite all the family to the wedding next week. After all, we missed the first one!' he bit out contemptuously.

She was immune to his insults, only one part of his accusation really meaning anything to her. 'Russell said the wedding is next week?'

'Don't tell me you didn't know!' Jordan bit out coldly.

Next week. She was supposed to become Russell's wife again *next week*, when it was the furious man standing before her that she loved.

CHAPTER EIGHT

JORDAN's anger faltered, then wavered as he saw the bewilderment in her eyes. 'You didn't know?' he said uncertainly. 'But that's stupid,' he added self-disgustedly. 'Of course you would know about your own wedding!'

Next week. It still didn't seem possible. Russell had said soon, but she still hadn't expected——
She couldn't marry Russell now. It had been difficult enough to contemplate before she had spent the night in Jordan's arms, before she had realised she was in love with him; now it was impossible.

'Well, say something, Willow,' rasped Jordan. 'Anything. Even if you only tell me it's the truth!'

Russell was taking no chances on her changing her mind if he had told his family, but she couldn't do it, she couldn't endure being married to him again. 'What was Simone's and David's reaction to the news?' she queried breathlessly.

Jordan's expression darkened. 'What about my reaction?' he bit out. 'The two of us spent all last night making love, and then before he and Gemma left this afternoon Russell calmly announced that the two of you were going to remarry!'

She swallowed hard. 'Russell left the island this afternoon?'

'Willow, did last night mean so little to you that you can ignore the fact that I'm furiously angry, totally bewildered—and hurting like hell!' He scowled as she looked at him with dazed eyes. 'I told you I was starting to care,' he snapped. 'Well, being together last night made sure of it.'

Did that mean he had fallen in love with her, too? Oh God, if only he had—— But it would achieve nothing but heartache for them both if he did; there was very little chance that she would be able to persuade Russell to change his mind about them remarrying, and even if she did he would never allow another man in her life, especially Jordan.

'When, exactly, did Russell leave Jersey?' she ignored the pain in the velvet brown eyes, her own heart feeling as if it were breaking.

'On the evening flight; I chartered my own plane,' he rasped. 'I needed to hear from your own lips that what Russell had said was true.' He frowned heavily. 'I think I now have my answer. But why, Willow?' He shook his head. 'You don't love him——'

'Jordan, I think this is between Russell and me,' she cut in pointedly.

'Last night gave me no rights at all?' His eyes were narrowed.

She turned away. 'None at all.'

He gave a snort of disgust. 'Then what was it for

you, one last fling before the shackles of matrimony smothered you again?'

Willow paled at his deliberate cruelty. 'Something like that,' she dismissed bitterly.

He drew in a harsh breath. 'And how do you think Russell would feel about his fiancée coming to my bed?' he scorned viciously, his hands clenched into fists at his sides.

Her breathing was uneven. 'Do you intend telling him about it?'

'No,' he scorned, his expression full of contempt as his gaze raked over her. 'I'm no more anxious for it to be known that I made a fool of myself over a scheming little bitch like you than you are to have people know you behaved like one!'

'Jordan!' Her choked cry halted him at the door, flinching back from the cold anger in his eyes as he swung around to look at her. 'I just want you to know, I—I will always remember last night.'

Fury blazed in the darkness of his eyes. 'Believe me, so will I!'

Even in his anger he remembered there was a child asleep in the house, closing the door quietly behind him as he left. As soon as the lock clicked shut Willow fell to the floor weeping.

'This isn't going to help anything.' Barbara briskly pulled her to her feet, gently seating her in an armchair.

Her eyes were like tear-wet emeralds as she looked up. 'You heard?'

'Most of it,' her friend admitted ruefully. 'He seemed pretty angry when he arrived, and so I——

You aren't really going through with this wedding, are you?' Barbara frowned worriedly.

'It's what Russell wants.'

'And what about what you want?' Barbara prompted impatiently. 'If I'm not mistaken, that's Jordan St James!'

The two of them hadn't discussed Willow's absence from their hotel suite last night, although from Barbara's speculative looks when she returned this morning she realised the other woman had guessed what had happened during those hours.

'History has proved time and time again that it isn't always possible to have what you want!'

'Don't be flippant,' Barbara dismissed, 'especially when I know you don't mean it. I'm right in supposing neither of you slept alone last night?' She quirked dark brows.

Delicate colour highlighted Willow's cheeks. 'We didn't sleep at all!'

'And tonight he's acting like a very jealous man——'

'An angry man,' she corrected heavily. 'He thinks I just used him last night.'

'Jealous,' Barbara maintained. 'Angry men pick up the telephone and hurl verbal abuse; jealous men make their accusations face to face. They also charter private planes to do it,' she added drily. 'I think Jordan St James is in love with you.'

'I hope not,' Willow trembled.

'Willow, even I can't believe you intend going through with this remarriage,' Barbara said disgustedly. 'Correction—especially me!'

'I don't,' she shook her head. 'I can't. Not after——' She broke off awkwardly. 'I just can't.'

'Of course you can't,' her friend dismissed briskly. 'So when are you going to tell Russell?'

It wasn't really a question of when, but how, and they both knew that. Russell agreeing to meekly accept her decision; telling him she had fallen in love with Jordan; it was out of the question.

Willow knew Russell's apartment well; it was the same one he had occupied before their marriage. Her nervousness was now increased by the fact that this was where Russell had chosen for them to meet.

She had telephoned his office first thing this morning, and he had suggested they go out to dinner tonight to discuss things. When she had turned down that idea, sure that neither of them would feel like eating when she had said what she had to, he put forward the idea of meeting at his apartment instead. It was even less appealing to her than the dinner idea, but at least it was private.

She had never liked the apartment, had found its ultra-modern furnishing, avant-garde paintings and sculptures totally out of place in a building that had been built during Victoria's reign. The previous time she had spent in the apartment with Russell had done little to endear the place to her.

Russell looked lithe and attractive when he opened the door to her ring, dressed casually in denims and a sweater a shade of blue that made his eyes appear darker, his expression one of boyish anticipation. 'Do you realise this is the first time you've made any move to see me for a very long time?' He opened the door wide in invitation, bending to kiss her lightly on the cheek as she passed him.

Willow flinched from his easy familiarity, her fingers tightening about her black clutch bag as she faced him across the cream and black lounge, her red dress a splash of colour in the starkness.

'Can I get you a drink?' he offered lightly.

'Russell, why did you tell your family that we're remarrying next week?' She came straight to the point, having no time for needless social pleasantries.

His eyes narrowed. 'My whole family, Willow?' he queried softly. 'Or just Jordan?'

She stiffened as he added the latter. 'What do you mean?'

'I'm sorry,' he drawled insincerely. 'I thought Jordan was the one to bring my announcement to your attention.' He quirked mocking brows.

Her mouth tightened at the taunt. 'Dani telephoned your parents this morning; Simone mentioned it to me then.' It was the truth, although she omitted to tell him that Jordan had 'mentioned it' first!

'I told you that even you look good to her now,' Russell derided, pouring himself a whisky.

Simone had been quite cordial about the remarriage, seeming to assume that seeing Russell with another woman had made Willow come to

her senses about him. The only time she had done
that had been when she had plucked up the
courage to leave him, and then later to divorce
him!

'Emerging the more preferable over Gemma
Laird doesn't exactly thrill me,' she scorned.

Russell gave a dismissive shrug. 'She always
gave me what you wouldn't.'

Willow paled at the accusation. 'Couldn't,' she
amended tightly.

His expression darkened. 'You didn't even try!'

Her breath shakily left her body. 'I did the best I
could.'

'Yes,' he derided hardly. 'And we both know
how good that was!'

Willow swallowed hard. 'It wouldn't be any
different a second time around.'

'No?'

She looked at him warily at the soft threat in his
voice. 'No,' she confirmed softly.

'Not even now you know what you've been
missing all these years?' he rasped tauntingly.

Her breath caught and held, her eyes narrowing. 'I have no idea——'

'Jordan!' he bit out contemptuously. 'He looked
as if someone had punched him when I announced
our wedding,' he said with satisfaction.

'I'm sure you're mistaken,' she dismissed. 'He
was probably just surprised.'

'It was surprise that made him fly over here to
see you yesterday, was it?' Russell rasped.

Her breathing stopped completely, although she

didn't know why she was so shocked that Russell knew of his cousin's visit; he had already admitted to having her watched. 'I think you would have to ask Jordan about that,' she said evasively.

'There's no need,' he dismissed derisively. 'I already know the reason.'

'You do?' Her eyes were wide with apprehension.

'Are you sure you wouldn't like a drink?' Russell offered pleasantly.

'No,' she snapped tautly. 'You know I hate these games you like to play!'

He raised his brows at her vehemence. 'You would prefer that I show you how I really feel about your spending the night with Jordan?' he said smoothly. 'I was trying to discuss it in a controlled and civilised way, something you always said I lacked. But if you would prefer my real feelings about it . . .' He shrugged broad shoulders.

'I think I will have that drink after all.' Willow sank down weakly into a chair. He *knew* she had slept with Jordan!

'I thought you might,' he drawled, pouring her a glass of whisky, adding the water he knew she preferred. 'Better?' he mocked when she had taken a sip.

'You——' She cleared her throat, swallowing with difficulty. 'You know about Jordan and me?'

'Yes.'

She drew in a ragged breath. 'How?'

'The same way I always know what you're

doing.' His voice was icy.

It hadn't even occurred to her that Russell would have her watched while she was on Jersey visiting his parents, believing that his presence there too would be enough to satisfy his curiosity this time. She should have known better! 'What are you going to do about it?' she looked at him anxiously.

'Nothing.'

'Nothing?' she repeated frowningly, not able to believe he would accept so calmly the knowledge that she had been to bed with another man.

He gave an abrupt inclination of his head. 'As long as I have your promise that it won't happen again.'

'It won't,' she said with certainty, sure that Jordan would never come near her again after yesterday.

'Don't be so quick to agree, Willow,' Russell taunted, relaxed as he stood in front of the unlit fireplace, central heating keeping the spacious apartment warm. 'I hadn't finished,' he explained hardly. 'I want your word that you will never allow Jordan to touch you again, yes. But I also want to know if you liked being in bed with him.'

She stood up agitatedly. 'I don't have to tell you that!' she blazed.

'Don't you?'

'No!'

'I've heard he's a very accomplished lover,' Russell rasped, his eyes narrowed.

Her head went back challengingly. 'I wouldn't

know, I have nothing to compare him with!' She
knew she had pushed him too far with this taunt as
his face paled, a white ring of tension about his
mouth, his hands clenching at his sides. 'Russell, I
didn't mean——'

'You knew exactly what you were saying,' he bit
out viciously, his eyes fiercely blue. 'But I was
never like that with any other woman but you. You
drive me insane!'

She could believe that, she knew there was
something about her that affected Russell in a way
that made him totally unreasonable, demanding
complete subjugation from her. In all things. It
had frightened and then terrified her all those
years ago. 'We aren't good for each other, Russell,'
she told him softly.

'Then you did enjoy Jordan's lovemaking!' he
accused harshly.

'Russell——'

'Why not mine, Willow?' He grasped her
roughly. 'Why do you only love my touch?' He
ground his mouth down on hers, demanding a
response from her, one he knew he would never
get.

Her hours with Jordan had increased her
contempt for Russell's caresses, and she felt
nauseated as the kiss went on and on, Russell being
determined to have a response from her before he
released her. Finally, out of desperation, she
returned the kiss, her mouth swollen, her eyes
clouded with tears as he savagely pushed her away
from him.

He thrust his hands into his denims' pockets. 'Do you love him?'

After being forced to endure this man's savagery she wasn't sure she could endure any of the species, tasting her own blood in her mouth where Russell has split her lip against her teeth. 'I don't know,' she answered truthfully, doubting the reality of Jordan's gentle lovemaking after Russell's attack on her senses.

'I told you to stay away from him,' Russell reminded her coldly.

'I——'

'Don't even attempt to lie to me, Willow,' he scorned harshly. 'I know you went straight to him after agreeing to remarry me.'

'You gave me no choice!' she gasped. 'There was no question of *agreeing*.'

'You wanted to be *asked*?' His chest rose and fell rapidly in his angry agitation. 'OK, Willow, I'm asking; will you marry me?'

'That's what I came here to talk to you about,' she returned tentatively.

'Yes?' he prompted gratingly, his belligerent gaze never leaving her pale face.

She moistened her lips with the tip of her tongue, feeling how swollen they were from his kisses. 'Surely neither of us really wants to live through that hell again?' She looked at him anxiously.

'Does that mean your answer is no?' he queried softly, too softly.

'It has to be, Russell,' she said pleadingly. 'We

can't live that way again. We——'

'I see,' he acknowledged gruffly.

She blinked at his calm, looking at him searchingly. 'You do?'

'Yes.' He nodded abruptly.

Willow breathed heavily, feeling as if she had just fought with a tiger—and then won because the tiger had decided *she* was the stronger! 'I mean it, Russell, I can't be your wife again.'

'I understand.'

She frowned her uncertainty. She had expected him to rant and rave, to threaten; not this—this calm. She didn't like it. 'I'm not sure that you do,' she began tentatively.

'I'm not stupid, Willow,' he rasped. 'I can understand when a woman is saying no to me.'

She knew he could understand it, he had just never accepted it from her before! It was a disquieting feeling after all these years to think that she might actually be allowed to live the rest of her life in peace. She didn't believe it!

'Russell, what sort of price are you going to exact for this?' She eyed him warily.

'Price?' he asked lightly.

'Yes—price.' She was so tense she felt as if she would snap in two if he didn't soon drop the axe she knew was about to fall. With Russell there was always a price for everything he did.

He shrugged his shoulders. 'I can't force you to remarry me.'

'Why not?' she said bitterly. 'You did the first time.'

His mouth twisted. 'Is that an invitation to get you pregnant again?'

'No!'

'I thought not.' He turned away, his hands still thrust into his trouser pockets. 'That appears to be that, then.'

She watched him uncertainly. It couldn't be this easy; saying no to him had never worked before. 'The wedding is off, then?'

He gave a terse inclination of his head. 'I just said so, didn't I?'

Willow swallowed hard, breathing shallowly. 'Russell, you won't——'

'For God's sake get out of here, Willow,' he grated suddenly, his face pale. 'We've said all that needs to be said!'

She stumbled to the door, glancing back at him anxiously before letting herself out of the apartment. Once outside she drew in a ragged breath, leaning back against the door. She had dreaded this meeting all day, and now she felt—curiously flat. And she didn't for one moment believe his calm acceptance of her decision; she knew him too well.

She certainly wasn't in the mood for a confrontation with Gemma Laird when she met her outside!

'Hello,' the other woman greeted her speculatively, her black dress moulded to her body, the high heels on her sandals making her appear even taller and more willowy. 'Have you been to see Russell?'

It was obvious from her dress and location that

the other woman had been about to do the same thing. Russell had invited Willow to his apartment while arranging to meet the other woman there, too? It didn't make sense, even for Russell.

'You're looking a little pale.' The other woman frowned. 'Are you all right?'

'Fine.' Willow dismissed her feelings of puzzlement; she had never been able to work out Russell's motives for anything he did.

'Are you sure?' Gemma persisted. 'We could go somewhere and have a coffee.'

'No, thank you.' She had no desire to discuss Russell with his mistress. 'I'm sure Russell must be expecting you.'

'Hm.' The other woman smiled. 'And I really shouldn't keep him waiting.' She turned to enter the building. 'Nice to have seen you again, Willow.'

Gemma Laird was either the most insensitive or the most bitchy woman Willow had ever met, and she couldn't make up her mind which it was!

'How did it go?' Barbara wanted to know as soon as Willow had let herself into the house.

'Surprisingly well. Dani?' She put her bag down wearily on the table, slipping off her shoes, a pensive frown marring the creamy smoothness of her brow.

'She hasn't stirred since you went out,' Barbara assured her dismissively. 'If your meeting with Russell went so well why are you looking so worried?' she asked shrewdly.

'I'm not sure,' she answered slowly. 'Except——' she broke off.

'Yes?' her friend prompted softly.

Willow shook her head. 'Maybe the remarriage was just a whim on his part,' she sighed.

'Did it seem like a whim at the time?' Barbara asked drily.

'No.' She shuddered. 'And I—he knows about the night I spent with Jordan,' she admitted worriedly.

'How—the person he has following you,' her friend realised. 'Maybe we should make some enquiries to see if we can find out who it is,' she frowned.

'That wouldn't stop Russell,' Willow said knowingly.

'Probably not,' Barbara conceded. 'But it is an infringement of privacy.'

'I haven't had a moment of that since I met Russell six years ago!'

'Then it's about time you did,' her friend decided firmly.

Willow knew, as did Barbara, that neither of them was really that worried about the person Russell had hired to follow her, that it was Russell's calm acceptance of her refusal to remarry him that bothered both of them.

Even though the next day was Saturday, and she didn't usually work at the weekends, this time she had no choice in the matter. She had been away for four days, and there was still so much to get ready for the fashion show which was fast looming on the horizon. Luckily it was a bright sunny day, and Barbara's suggestion that she and Dani go to the park was greeted enthusiastically by an excited Dani.

'Make sure you keep wrapped up,' Willow cautioned her impatient daughter. 'It's cold out there, in spite of the sunshine.'

'I will, Mummy,' Dani humoured her, a mischievous twinkle in her eyes. 'Don't forget to join us for lunch.'

She just had a couple of fittings to do this morning, and she hoped that wouldn't take more than a couple of hours. She was sure she would be finished in time to join them for lunch. 'Be a good girl for Barbara.' She buttoned up Dani's coat.

'I always am.' Dani skipped over to the other woman's side, her hand trustingly in hers.

'Oh, she is,' Barbara agreed drily. 'Don't work too hard!'

That was easier said than done. Everything seemed to conspire against her that morning; she had trouble getting a taxi to her studio, then one of the models was late arriving and the other one ripped the side of one of the gowns as she pulled it on over her head. Thank God this only happened once a year; she couldn't live through it any more than that!

'Can we go now?' Shirlee finally sighed. 'I'm meeting someone for lunch.'

Lunch? Willow looked quickly down at her wristwatch: ten to one. She should have met

Barbara and Dani twenty minutes ago!

'Make sure you're both in nice and early on Monday,' she warned, quickly packing away, anxious to be gone herself.

It really was a beautiful day, the sun shining brightly even though there was a wintry nip in the air, birds singing from tree-tops and houses. She just hoped Barbara and Dani hadn't got too cold waiting for her in the park; Dani was very prone to colds at this time of year.

She came to an abrupt halt as she turned the corner to their meeting spot to see several policeman standing with Barbara as she gestured wildly as she talked.

The colour drained from Willow's face, and she hurried towards them, running by the time she reached them, her own heartbeat thundering in her ears.

Barbara's eyes were full of tears as she turned to look at her, a trickle of blood at her temple.

'Dani?' Willow managed to choke.

'He took her, Willow,' Barbara exclaimed emotionally. 'He's got Dani!'

CHAPTER NINE

WILLOW had seen news articles like this on the television, and her heart had gone out to the parents of the abducted child, thankful that her own daughter was safely tucked up in bed. She had never realised how totally heartbreaking it was to know that your child had been taken from you, that you were impotent to do anything about getting her back again.

The same doctor who came to the house to examine the blow Barbara had taken to the head prescribed tranquillisers for Willow, but she refused to take anything that would dull her senses. Dani had been abducted, and she intended being completely conscious and alert until she had her back again. *Then* she would collapse.

The police had listened while they told them that Dani's father had taken her, wanting a complete description of Dani anyway, and of what she had been wearing. It hadn't been at all difficult to picture Dani as she had looked before going out this morning, her gamine features alight with mischief, looking like a little pixie in the red bobble-hat and matching gloves with her navy blue anorak, denims, and a bright red jumper worn beneath the coat.

Barbara had explained that they had been

sitting on the bench waiting for Willow when she had been hit from behind. When she regained consciousness, Dani had gone.

'We'll get her back,' Barbara assured the numbed Willow once the police had finished their questioning and gone to call at Russell's apartment.

'Will we?' Willow looked at her with dull eyes, noting the gauze pad now plastered to the cut at her temple. 'Oh, Barbara, I shouldn't have been late! I shouldn't have been at work at all! What sort of mother am I anyway, to go——'

'Self-recrimination, when you have nothing to blame yourself for, isn't going to help anyone,' her friend said briskly. 'I was in charge of Dani; I was the one who let Russell take her.'

'You didn't exactly let him.' Willow looked pointedly at the other woman's injury. 'I should never have left Dani today——'

'You couldn't have known what was going to happen,' Barbara soothed.

'Couldn't I?' she said bitterly, thinking of the trepidation she had known when Russell had been so calm the night before. She should have held on to that feeling, stayed with Dani every minute of the day. 'The police actually seemed relieved once they realised it was a "domestic dispute"!'

'Well, he is Dani's father; he isn't likely to hurt her.'

Russell had never raised a hand against Dani, but that didn't mean he wouldn't start now if things didn't go his way. He——

'Willow, we have to let the Stewarts know,' Barbara gently cut in on her traumatic thoughts. 'Dani is their granddaughter.'

Willow stood up, pacing the room. 'You think they don't already know?' she scorned. 'Dani could be with them right now!'

Barbara frowned. 'I don't think Russell would take her there.'

One thing neither of them doubted, Russell had been the one to hit Barbara and take Dani!

The retribution Willow had been expecting had been brutal and sudden, and made against the person who had always been totally innocent of any wrong: Dani. But Russell had always known that their daughter was her weak spot, and that was where he had struck.

'Perhaps not,' she conceded, sure that David, if not Simone, would never put her though this agony of heart and mind. 'But he has her somewhere, I know it!'

'Yes,' Barbara agreed abruptly. 'Shall I call the Stewarts or will you?'

She drew in a ragged breath. 'You do it. I—I can't talk to them just now. But don't take too long; Russell may try and telephone me with his conditions for bringing Dani back!'

'I had to involve the police, you do realise that?' Barbara frowned. 'Russell is unstable.'

'I've always known that,' she quivered. 'Please, hurry!'

She stared out of the window while Barbara made the call, not interested in the conversation,

watching as a car went by the house, a man walked
his dog, a couple of teenagers giggled together; the
world was going on about its business quite
normally while Dani had been taken from her!
She had no doubt that Russell's method of taking
her would have frightened her daughter; she
didn't really know her father that well, and he had
hurt her beloved Barbara. She only hoped that
Dani didn't anger him.

'Mrs Stewart took the call,' Barbara told her
after ringing off. 'She went hysterical the moment
I told her about Dani being taken, and then Mr St
James came on the line; apparently Mr Stewart
had gone into town.'

'Jordan?' Willow trembled just at the mention
of his name.

'He said they'll be here in a couple of hours,' her
friend told her briskly.

She hadn't thought they would actually want to
come here; she wasn't sure she could cope with
any of them. 'Oh, Barbara, if he harms her . . .' She
shuddered at the thought.

'He won't,' Barbara said with certainty. 'He
wouldn't have anything to bargain with if he did.'

Marriage for returning Dani safely. Yes, she
knew that would be the deal Russell had in mind.
Their first marriage had been a succession of such
deals. First marriage? Had she already accepted
the fact that she would agree to anything he asked
of her? What choice did she really have? She had
said no to him once and this had been his reaction.

Both she and Barbara jumped to their feet a few

minutes later when the doorbell rang, Willow frowning her puzzlement when she saw Gemma Laird standing outside. Unless Russell had sent a message through her——

'Where is she?' Willow demanded fiercely. 'Tell me or I'll——'

'I saw the police,' Gemma Laird faltered. 'I—is something wrong?'

Her bewilderment was so genuine that Willow knew the other woman had no idea what was going on. She turned away dejectedly, going back into the lounge to wait by the telephone, her eyes widening as Barbara brought the other woman through a few minutes later. 'I don't feel in the mood for company right now——'

'I think you should hear this,' Barbara grated, looking expectantly at Gemma Laird.

The other woman looked very uncomfortable. 'I didn't know,' she shook her head. 'I had no idea. Russell told me——'

'You know where Dani is?' Willow pounced, her eyes bright.

'No,' Gemma Laird said regretfully. 'I had no idea Russell had taken her until just now. But I— He told me he wanted you watched to make sure you didn't try to leave the country with Dani.'

'Why should I want to leave the country with her? I had custody of her—— *You're* the person Russell hired to follow me?' gasped Willow.

Bright spots of colour highlighted the other woman's cheeks. 'Yes.'

'But the two of you are lovers,' she accused.

'Yes, we became so,' Gemma admitted shakily. 'I—I loved him.'

'And do you still love him?' scorned Willow. 'Now that you know he's terrorising his own child so that he can have what he really wants: me!'

Gemma swallowed convulsively. 'he told me that it was Dani he wanted, that he deeply regretted giving you custody of her, that you knew that, and that he feared you might take Dani away so that he could never see her again.'

'And you believed him?' she said with distaste.

Blue eyes flashed resentfully. 'You wouldn't be the first couple to disagree over the custody of your child.'

'You would know a lot about that in your line of work!'

'Willow!' Barbara admonished.

'Couldn't you see how little real interest Russell had in Dani?' Willow was unrelenting as she attacked the woman who had been paid to spy on her.

'I didn't——'

'Willow, I don't think this conversation is helping the situation at all,' Barbara began.

'It's helping *me*,' she snapped, moving agitatedly about the room. 'Do you enjoy spying on people, Miss Laird,' she sneered. 'I must have been pretty boring stuff,' she continued scornfully before Gemma Laird could reply. 'Until Jersey. Then things hotted up a bit, didn't they?' she said contemptuously.

'I——'

'Did you sneak up to Jordan's house and try to see the two of us together through the window or did you just sit outside all night drawing your own conclusions?' She looked at the other woman with distaste.

Gemma Laird was very pale, her make-up a livid mask against that pallor. 'Russell hired me to report on your comings and goings, not to guess at what you might be doing at a certain place.'

'I stayed the whole night at a man's house and you didn't draw *any* conclusions?' Willow said disbelievingly. 'Because Russell did,' she rasped. 'It's the reason he's taken Dani!'

Gemma Laird swallowed hard. 'He hasn't tried to contact you?'

She drew in a ragged breath. 'Not yet. But he will,' she said with certainty.

'I don't understand this.' The other woman shook her head. 'If Russell still—loves you——'

'Oh, believe me, he does.' Willow nodded abruptly. 'At least, it's what he calls love. I have another, much different, name for it,' she added bitterly.

'Then why didn't he fight the divorce, why stay away from you the last year?'

'It's a long story,' Willow said flatly. 'And one I'm not willing to tell you.'

Gemma Laird frowned. 'I suppose you are sure it is Russell who has kidnapped your daughter? Dani comes from a very rich family, and kidnapping has become more common in England in recent years.'

'Russell has her,' said Willow with calm certainty. 'Yesterday I refused to remarry him.'

'But——'

'There can be no doubt, Miss Laird.' Barbara took over forcefully, 'Russell has her. And if you have any idea where he might have taken her I think you should tell us now.'

'I don't. I—have you tried the most obvious place, his apartment?' Gemma frowned.

'The police were going straight there; they would have come back to us by now if they had found them,' Barbara explained grimly.

Gemma nodded. 'I can't think of anywhere else ... I really am sorry, Willow.' She looked at her anxiously. 'I had no idea he planned to do anything like this.'

'I suppose you were the one who told him Dani and Barbara had gone to the park without me this morning?' Willow said scathingly.

The other woman gave a pained grimace. 'Yes.'

'And when we met outside Russell's apartment last night, were you spying on me then, too?'

'Yes.'

'It was quick thinking on your part to pretend to be going to see Russell. Or did I just assume that?' Willow frowned at her stupidity. 'Would you have just waited outside his apartment all night if I'd allowed him to blackmail me into staying?' she derided coldly.

'Willow,' Barbara reproved gently, 'can't you see Miss Laird is almost as shocked by this as you are?'

Willow looked properly at the other woman for the first time, finally seeing how ill she looked; the expertly applied make-up did nothing to hide her years now. 'I'm sorry,' she said heavily. 'You're to be pitied for loving a bastard like Russell.'

'I think you'd better go now,' Barbara prompted the other woman, accompanying her to the door as she slowly complied.

Willow leant her head back in the chair, the tears falling silently from beneath her closed lids. Dani . . . Oh God, Dani, where are you? She was gripped with panic every time she envisaged her daughter's bewilderment. Oh, she could *kill* Russell with her bare hands for doing this!

'Oh, love, don't torture yourself like this.' Barbara came down on her knees in front of her chair. 'He'll bring her back, you'll see.'

'He was so calm when I told him I wouldn't marry him,' Willow remembered, her eyes wide and staring, but seeing nothing. 'He took it so well—too well. I should have known——'

'Willow, you have to stay calm,' Barbara told her in a stern voice as hysteria threatened. 'You have to be strong, for Dani's sake. She's going to want a smiling, unruffled mother when she gets home.'

She knew Barbara was talking sense, but it didn't really help. She couldn't be happy again until she had Dani back in her arms. Nevertheless, she let Barbara make her a cup of tea, knowing the other woman needed to be kept busy, that she still blamed herself for letting Dani be taken.

But the seconds, the minutes, and finally the hours passed, and there was still no word from Russell. And as the time slowly dragged past Willow was filled with more and more recriminations. Why had she even tried to fight Russell? He always won in the end.

When the doorbell rang almost two hours later she came abruptly to her feet, knowing who it was; Jordan had telephoned from the airport to let them know he and the Stewarts were on their way to her house. Willow had received a jolt when Barbara had told her he was with Simone and David, although knowing Jordan as she now did she should have realised he wouldn't have callously stayed on Jersey.

It was to his face her stricken gaze went as they came into the room and she ran to him instinctively as she saw the worry and the compassion etched there. His arms opened to her as with a choked sob she gave vent to all the despair she had been holding in check the last few hours as she waited.

'Jordan!' his aunt's shocked voice rasped.

'Can I get you all a cup of tea?' Barbara offered quietly.

'You can tell me what you were doing while someone walked off with my granddaughter.' Simone turned on her accusingly, her blue eyes blazing, her usual control gone.

'I——'

'Simone,' Willow roused herself enough to admonish, although she wasn't strong enough to leave the haven of Jordan's arms. 'Barbara isn't to blame for what happened.'

'Then who is?' Simone attacked, not at all her usual impeccable self, lines etched into her beautiful face, drastically ageing her. 'Miss Gibbons told us she was with Dani when she was taken——'

'She was. But——'

'Then she should have taken better care of my granddaughter,' Simone accused. 'She——'

'Barbara is the best care Dani *could* have had in the circumstances,' Willow told her quietly, avoiding the gentle probing of Jordan's gaze, although she still clung to him. 'She has been Dani's bodyguard for the last three years.'

'Bodyguard?' Simone repeated caustically. 'Why on earth would Dani need a bodyguard?' she dismissed. 'And where is Russell?' she demanded to know. 'The poor boy must be worried out of his mind!'

Willow shot Barbara a startled look.

The other woman shrugged ruefully. 'The telephone didn't seem the best place to tell them.' She grimaced.

'Tell us what?' Simone's gaze sharpened suspiciously. 'Willow, what——?'

'Simone, I think it would be better if we all just calmed down,' Jordan put in softly, his arm still about Willow's waist as he guided her to the sofa, sitting down at her side. 'Willow has had a tremendous shock, and——'

'Haven't we all?' snapped Simone. 'She——'

'Simone,' David's voice was quietly authorita-
tive. 'Let's just sit down and let Willow explain
this to us in her own way.'

Simone did so with ill grace, perched on the
edge of her chair, her movements agitated. 'Why
isn't Russell here?' she rasped impatiently. 'Don't
tell me you haven't told him!'

'Oh, he knows about it,' Willow nodded dully,
her eyes pained.

'Then why isn't he here?' Simone's voice rose
shrilly. 'Don't tell me the two of you have argued
again. You were always arguing——'

'Simone, Russell isn't here because he's the one
who has Dani,' Willow cut in quietly, keeping her
back against Jordan's chest as his arm tightened
about her painfully. She didn't dare look at him,
frightened that she might see the same shocked
disbelief that was in Simone's face reflected in his,
drawing from his stength and warmth when she
felt like collapsing. She could understand Barbara's reluctance to tell Simone on the telephone about Russell's involvement, knew that
the other woman wouldn't have believed her.
As she didn't now.

'Don't be absurd!' Simone scorned. 'He would
never worry us all like this.'

'Mrs Stewart, your son does have Dani,'
Barbara insisted firmly.

'How would you know?' Simone blazed. 'You
claim someone knocked you unconscious, so I
don't see how you could possibly know what
happened to Dani. You probably weren't hit at all

but had fallen asleep, and Dani wondered off. Russell would never take Dani off like this without telling Willow. I think you're just trying to cover up for your own incompetence. You could even have been meeting some man, and——'

'Simone, that's enough!' Willow ordered shakily. 'Barbara is a trained bodyguard; she would never have taken her eyes off Dani while she was in her care. I don't think you're really listening to what we're trying to tell you. Barbara isn't saying that Russell met Dani in the park and took her off for an ice-cream or something! He has deliberately taken Dani away from me, and he knocked Barbara unconscious to do it!'

At last she dared a look at Jordan. The last time they had met he had been angry and accusing; now his eyes glowed with another emotion, and his hand was gentle against her cheek as he smoothed away the dampness of her tears.

'My son isn't capable of hurting anyone,' Simone bit out forcefully.

'No?' Barbara challenged softly. 'I don't think he knows how to do anything else!'

'Barbara, no!' Willow warned desperately as she guessed what the other woman was about to say.

Her friend looked at her with compassionate grey eyes. 'They have to be told, Willow,' she insisted gently. 'It's time.'

'No!' she gasped.

'It may be the only way Russell can be stopped,' Barbara prompted.

Willow knew that, but she couldn't, she *couldn't*!

'Tell us, Barbara,' Jordan prompted softly, his eyes narrowed and unfathomable.

'Tell us what?' Simone said disparagingly. 'More lies about Russell?'

'They aren't lies, Mrs Stewart.' Barbara told her regretfully.

'Jordan, you can't mean to listen to this?' Simone gasped disbelievingly.

'I think it's time we all heard the truth,' David put in softly.

'David!' His wife turned on him. 'They mean to tell more lies about our son!'

'Are they lies?' he frowned.

'Of course they are,' his wife snapped, 'to excuse their neglect of Dani.'

David shook his head. 'Willow never neglected Dani. In fact, you used to complain she spent more time with her than she did with Russell.'

Simone flushed. 'A proper wife and mother knows how to divide her time between the two!'

He gave an ackowledging inclination of his head. 'But while they were married I can never remember Willow looking at Russell with anything but fear and disgust.'

Simone gasped her outrage. 'Then why should she agree to remarry him if she feared him?'

'I think that's what we're just about to find out,' David said heavily. 'Russell is my son, and because he is I love him, but even when he was a child I remember that he would rather smash up a favourite toy than share it with anyone.'

'As you said, he was a child,' Simone dismissed impatiently. 'I don't see what that has to do with what's happening now.'

'Don't you?' her husband sighed. 'Maybe not. Although I don't think I was the only one who noticed how close Willow and Jordan were becoming during her stay on the island. Was I, my dear?' he prompted Willow.

'No.' Tears glistened unshed in her eyes at his understanding.

'This is ridiculous,' Simone snapped impatiently. 'She and Russell were going to remarry!'

'Were you?' David held Willow's gaze gently.

She swallowed hard. 'No, I told him I couldn't marry him.' She heard Jordan's sharp intake of breath, turning to look at him with pleading eyes.

He looked at her, searching, before turning to Barbara once again. 'Tell us, Barbara,' he prompted again in a husky voice.

'Yes,' snapped Simone, 'tell us what Russell did to hurt Willow when she was the one to leave him, to take his child from him!'

Willow paled, unable to answer that herself, and her nails dug into the palm of Jordan's hand as she gripped it.

'A child,' Barbara began, 'that Willow loves more than life itself; a child that exists because your son raped her, savagely and intentionally, because a pregnancy would ensure that she married him when she had already refused him!'

CHAPTER TEN

'I DON'T believe it!' Simone stood up indignantly. 'It's a lie, all lies to cover up the fact that *she* tricked my son into marriage!'

Willow's head was bowed, and numbly she acknowledged that her nails had pierced Jordan's skin, that he was even now wrapping a snowy white handkerchief with studied concentration about the three half-moon puncture marks as they seeped blood.

Rape. Such an ugly word; such an ugly deed. And it had been ugly, painful, both mentally and physically.

Russell had asked her to marry him on their third date, but by that time she had known she didn't love him, that she had only been dazzled by his maturity and sophistication. She had been seventeen, barely out of school, easily flattered by his attention. He had been stunned by her refusal to marry him, although he had recovered well, inviting her out to dinner, just as a friend. She had agreed because she felt guilty about turning him down, although she had baulked a little when he had taken her back to his apartment after dinner.

What followed had been the most horrific experience imaginable, with Russell telling her she was his, and that he was going to have her, even as he ripped through the barrier of her innocence and claimed her. She had been too ashamed of what had happened to even tell her parents.

Five weeks later she had known she was pregnant.

She had been terrified, completely panicked as she wondered what would become of her. She needn't have worried about that; her parents had been overjoyed when she had finally confessed her condition to them, dismissing what she told them of her rape as being her guilty conscience for 'being a naughty girl'. They had insisted on telephoning Russell and congratulating him on his expected fatherhood.

After that, everything had moved so fast, with Russell elated that his forced lovemaking had produced such an effective result. When Willow had still refused to marry him he had bought her parents a larger house and promoted her father several steps up his career ladder. When she had continued to refuse, he had used her unborn child to force her into it. He had forced her to do everything during their marriage, none of the times he came to her body being as violent as that first one, but never receiving a response either. How could she respond to the man who had raped her!

'He said,' her voice was husky with pain, 'that if the first time hadn't produced a result he would have taken me again and again until it had.' She looked at no one, talking to herself, remembering, still ashamed of what had happened to her.

'What woman would marry the man who raped her?' Simone dismissed derisively.

Willow looked up then, feeling hot all over as rage consumed her. 'I wasn't a woman, I was a seventeen-year-old girl with very ambitious parents!' She stood up. 'I had nothing and no one but them, and they wanted me to marry Russell!'

'And you didn't?' the other woman scoffed.

'Want to marry a man who took me against my will every night of our marriage?' Her eyes were like huge emeralds in her pale face. 'Who subjugated me totally by threatening to expose my child as the result of his rape? My beautiful Dani going through life with that stigma attached to her?' She shuddered. 'I would have put up with anything, even Russell's constant abuse, to save my child from that!'

'Russell wouldn't—he didn't——'

'Yes, he did.' She cut across Simone's stumbling refusal to accept the truth. 'Oh, I tried to be a wife to him, to make the best of what we had, but every time he came near me I remembered the way he'd raped me. I couldn't respond to him, but he would take me anyway. A year after Dani was born I knew I couldn't take any more, and I think what he had become sickened him too, because he let me go.'

'On condition that you let him visit you once a week,' Barbara put in hardly.

Willow's cheeks were fiery red. 'Yes, on that condition. He gave me custody of Dani at the divorce on the same condition, but——' She looked at Jordan as he drew in a harsh breath. He looked angry, furiously angry. 'He never visited me after the divorce.' She bowed her head so that she didn't have to see the condemnation in Jordan's eyes. What she had done disgusted him. 'Last week he told me why he hadn't,' she said shakily. 'He'd given me a year to miss him before we became husband and wife again. Miss him?' she repeated harshly. 'I hate him, I've always hated him!'

'I—Jordan, where are you going?' his bewildered aunt demanded of him as he stood up to stride over to the door.

His eyes were as cold as ice as he half turned. 'Out,' he rasped.

'But——'

'I'll be back.' His gaze sought and held Willow's. 'I promise,' he added grimly, and the door closed decisively behind him.

'Well!' Simone said exasperatedly. 'Isn't it typical of a man to walk out at a time like this? He——' With her usual grace of movement she sank to the floor, unconscious as she hit the carpet.

The faint was such a surprise that for a moment Willow could only watch wide-eyed as David and Barbara bent over the unconscious woman.

David looked up at her with tortured eyes, suddenly older than his years. 'I'm sorry, Willow.' He spoke gruffly. 'I knew you weren't happy with Russell, but I had no idea . . .' He closed his eyes briefly. 'Simone knows you're telling the truth.' He held his wife's hand in his much larger one. 'She just won't accept it yet.'

Willow knelt beside him, worried by the other woman's pallor. 'Shall I call a doctor?'

'No.' David swung her up into his arms. 'If I could just put her to bed for a while . . .'

'Of course. I——'

'I'll take them,' Barbara offered as Willow looked lost. 'You just sit down until I get back.'

Willow sat, reacting to instructions now. Her marriage to Russell had been a nightmare she had just been forced to live through again as she told the Stewarts. And Jordan. He had looked disgusted by what she had allowed her life to become; he couldn't bear to be in the same room with her.

She couldn't really blame him. She had disgusted herself many times during her marriage to Russell. His love for her was obsessive, sick, and after a year and a half of sharing a bed with him she hadn't been able to stay with him another day longer. He had pleaded with her to come back, but by that time she had employed Barbara to protect Dani, only agreeing to meet his demand that he be allowed to see her once a week, just grateful that he hadn't asked anything else of her. As usual it had been Dani he had used to get her to agree, dismissing her claim that he would suffer more than anyone if he made public Dani's conception during his rape of her; they both knew Dani was the one who would be talked about and speculated over. One night a week in his arms hadn't seemed too high a price for his silence, not after all that had gone before it. And so for two years he had accepted their living arrangements, at least having her co-operation in bed now, if not her response.

One single night with Jordan had shown her just how sickening she had always found Russell's lovemaking.

And Jordan was disgusted with her now that he knew the truth. But he hadn't lived with the constant fear she had, couldn't understand weakness when he was so strong. She had done the only thing she could do, had no one to turn to for help.

'Willow.'

She slowly turned to look at David, her eyes glistening with tears.

'Barbara is going to sit with Simone until she wakes up,' he told her huskily. 'Willow, I—I'm sorry for what my son did to you.' His eyes were clouded with pain. 'For what he's still doing to you.'

She sighed raggedly. 'There are some people who would say I brought it on myself——'

'*No one* would say you brought that on yourself.' David thrust his shaking hands in his trouser pockets. 'Russell was always so possessive about things and people. He was only a year old when Jordan came to live with us, and yet for months he made our life hell. We bought him things to make up for it, and we never had any more children of our own in case he reacted the same way with them. Maybe that was where we went wrong——'

'You didn't make Russell the way he is!'

'It has to start somewhere, Willow,' he insisted

grimly. 'He was thoroughly spoilt as a child, so
much so that by the time he reached adolescence
he was totally uncontrollable, believed he could
have anything he wanted. He usually managed to
get it by persuasion and charm, but on the few
occasions he didn't his temper was something to
be reckoned with.' He shook his head. 'None of us
had the least suspicion of what he'd done to you.'

'Why should you?' she shrugged. 'I married
him.'

'You were only a child,' David groaned. 'And
your parents—God, if you'd been my daughter I
would have killed Russell, not welcomed him into
the family!'

She gave a wan smile. 'You have to know my
parents to understand them. They had a pregnant
daughter by my father's employer, a man who
wanted to marry me. And I don't think they ever
really believed Russell raped me,' she added
heavily. 'He was always so charming around
them.'

'That doesn't excuse——'

'—them forcing me into marriage,' she finished
derisively. 'I never thought so either. Which is
why I see as little of them as possible. Is Simone
going to be all right, do you think?' She abruptly
changed the subject; her parents' betrayal was still
very painful for her.

'It's been a shock,' David excused. 'To all of us.
You and Jordan——'

'There is no Jordan and I,' she cut in hardly.
'Especially now.'

'Jordan is a good man——'

'Not good enough to accept that I married and stayed with the man who had raped me!'

'Don't underestimate him, Willow.' David shook his head. 'He was angry just now, but not at you.'

It wasn't Jordan's anger she feared, it was his disgust and contempt for what she had done. And he had shown her both emotions by walking out the way he had.

'Russell took Dani to make you remarry him, didn't he?' his father said heavily.

'Yes.'

'And?'

She swallowed hard. 'I think I'll go up and check on Simone.' She made a hurried exit up the stairs, shaking so badly she paused halfway up them to steady herself. Telling Russell's family about what he had done to her had done nothing to ease the guilt and shame she still felt over the rape and the marriage that had followed. If anything she felt worse.

'Any news?' Barbara turned to her anxiously, in the chair by the bed where Simone lay.

'None,' Willow shook her head. 'How is she?' She looked concernedly at Simone.

'She woke up a little while ago and I gave her the tranquillisers the doctor gave me for you,' Barbara admitted ruefully. 'She was a little hysterical. But as you can see, she's sleeping now.'

'Perhaps it's as well,' Willow grimaced.

'How are you bearing up?' Barbara watched her closely.

She shrugged. 'I feel as if I've just been violated again, but I'll survive. It's Dani I'm worried about.'

'Mr Stewart seems like a sensible man,' Barbara remarked conversationally.

'He is,' Willow nodded abruptly. 'He—he believes me about Russell. Maybe I should have told him long ago; I think he would have helped me.'

'You've bottled it up inside you for so long now I didn't think you would ever tell anyone. Even if it cost you your happiness a second time around.' Barbara looked at her searchingly.

'You saw Jordan's reaction,' she bit out.

'Murderous,' Barbara nodded.

'Disgust,' Willow corrected gruffly.

'Willow, you——' Barbara broke off as the sound of smashing crockery came up the stairs. 'I think your guest needs a little help,' she said drily.

David was standing in the middle of the kitchen surrounded by two shattered cups and saucers. 'I thought I'd make us all a cup of tea. I—I'm sorry.' He began to pick up the pieces.

Willow knelt to help him, impulsively clasping one of his shaking hands. 'It will be all right,' she assured him. 'Dani will be home soon.'

He looked at her with tortured eyes. 'If my son harms her—I'll kill him!' he ground out.

'You'll have to stand in line,' Jordan rasped harshly. 'Willow, would you——?'

'Dani!' She had eyes only for the tiny figure that stood in front of him, scrambling to her feet to rush across the room and hold her bewildered daughter in her arms. 'Dani—Dani! Oh, darling, are you all right?' She was crying and laughing at the same time, touching her daughter all over just to make sure she was real and not some hallucination of her tortured heart.

'Oh, Mummy!' A tiny tear-wet face was pressed into her neck. 'Daddy hurt Barbara, and ——'

'Barbara is fine, darling,' she quickly assured her distressed daughter. 'She's upstairs right now with Grandma.'

Dani looked at her grandfather shyly before burying her face in Willow's neck once more.

'Jordan, where did you—how did you——'

'Why don't you take Dani upstairs and give her a nice bath?' he suggested gently. 'We can talk later.'

'But——'

'Please, Willow.' He looked pointedly at Dani. 'She's had something to eat, and she looks sleepy.'

Dani was the only reality to her as she carried her up the stairs, talking to her softly all the way, assuring her that she was safe now. She didn't know how or where Jordan had found Dani, she was just grateful that he had.

Dani cried all over again once she had seen for herself that Barbara was indeed alive and well, then let Willow carry her off to the bathroom with the promise of being allowed to use the jacuzzi.

'Daddy took me to where he works.' Dani began

to chatter once she was in the water surrounded by the bubbles she loved. 'He showed me how to press the buttons on the computers. And we had sandwiches and juice from a machine. But I knew you and Barbara would be worried about me, because I hadn't told you where I was going. And Daddy hit Barbara——'

'It was an accident, darling,' lied Willow, her eyes glowing as she looked her fill of her beautiful daughter. She was never going to let anything hurt or distress her ever again.

'But he hurt her——'

'Only a little,' she comforted, desperately trying to diminish the nightmare of the day in Dani's mind, realising how badly it could affect her if she realised the terrible danger she had really been in. 'Like you did when you shut the door on Mummy's fingers.'

'He was naughty,' Dani decided obstinately. 'And I didn't like being in the big building. Or having sandwiches for lunch and tea. I was very pleased when Uncle Jordan arrived.'

Willow doubted Russell had been. It hadn't occurred to her that Russell would take her to his office building, although for that very reason it was an ideal choice. Thank heavens Jordan had thought of it. She couldn't help wondering where Russell was now.

'I'm sure you were, sweetheart.' She wrapped Dani in a towel as she held her fiercely in her arms.

'Can I have some milk and biscuits?' Dani asked wheedlingly.

Willow's brow cleared as she realised the experience of being taken by her father had been nowhere near as traumatic for Dani as it had for the rest of them, although she seriously doubted they would escape without some reaction to the abduction. 'Of course you can, darling,' she smiled. 'I'll go and get them for you——'

'Couldn't Barbara go?' Dani clung to her, looking very small and vulnerable in her pretty pink cotton nightgown.

Willow's smile remained firmly fixed in place, although her eyes were shadowed. 'Let's go and ask her.'

Half an hour later Dani had consumed the biscuits and milk, listened to two stories, and sat on her mother's knee to be rocked to sleep, something she hadn't done since she was a baby.

Tears glistened in Willow's eyes as she gazed down at the sleeping angel she held, her arms tightening protectively. Russell would never come near Dani again. Never, she vowed fiercely.

'Willow,' Barbara called to her softly from the doorway. 'They want you downstairs. I'll sit with Dani,' she offered as Willow went to protest. 'Mrs Stewart looks as if she's out for the night!'

Willow reluctantly laid her daughter down on her bed, pausing to smooth back the silver-blonde hair from her face. 'If he had harmed her——'

'But he didn't,' Barbara cut in smoothly. 'Now don't worry, I won't leave her.'

She left the room with a backward glance at her daughter, knowing she had to talk to Jordan, but loath to leave the daughter she had feared would never be returned to her.

She hadn't expected to face Russell when she opened the lounge door!

One of his eyes showed signs of discoloration, his nose was bloody, and his mouth was swollen on one side. Someone had beaten him up—and recently.

Willow's gaze swung across the room to Jordan. He looked as controlled as ever, but there was a bruise on his cheek that hadn't been there before, and the knuckles on his right hand looked red and sore.

'Is Dani all right?' he prompted softly.

'Yes. But—what happened here?' she frowned.

'Your lover beat me up,' Russell sneered.

She gasped, looking uncomfortably at David. It was one thing to think there was a relationship between her and Jordan, quite another to have it put into words so bluntly. Although she had her answer as to where Russell was. And she knew that Jordan had waited until Dani was safely out of earshot before punishing the other man for what he had done.

'Don't worry.' David looked grim. 'I'm certainly not condemning you for trying to find happiness with someone else after what my son put you through.'

'What *I* put her through?' Blue eyes widened with innocent query.

'Willow told us everything,' his father rasped with distaste.

'Well, I wish someone would tell me,' Russell returned lightly. 'The first I realised anything was wrong was when my grim-faced cousin burst into my office after persuading my security man to let him in and told me he was taking Dani home. I——'

'It's all right, Jordan.' David calmed him as he took a threatening step towards his cousin, moving to stand directly in front of his son. 'I wish I'd let Jordan kill you a few moments ago instead of just hurting you a little. You deserve it for what you made Willow suffer over the years!'

Russell had lost some of his colour; he was not looking quite as sure of himself as usual, either. 'I don't know what—— Mother!' His gaze was fixed on the rumpled woman who stood in the doorway. 'What happened to you?' He frowned his concern.

All eyes were riveted on the tiny woman as she swayed slightly where she stood.

Simone suddenly looked old to Willow, old and frail, although that impression was instantly dispelled as she met Willow's gaze with fierce blue eyes.

CHAPTER ELEVEN

RUSSELL instantly moved to his mother's side. 'Mother, you——'

'Don't touch me!' she cried, shaking his hands off her as if he burnt her, one of her own hands arching up to slap him a stinging blow across one cheek. 'You're an animal!'

'What——?'

'You disgust me!' She glared at her stunned son with dislike.

Russell was more taken aback by the attack than any of them, lifting a hand to rub his throbbing cheek, his face having lost all its colour except for the bruising he had so recently received.

Willow had watched the scene with widely disbelieving eyes, so sure that Simone believed in her son's innocence, despite what David had said earlier to the contrary; she was sure Russell believed that, too.

'Has anyone called the police?' Simone demanded, in control of herself again.

'Not yet.' Jordan looked at her with narrowed eyes. 'We weren't sure——'

'Call them now,' his aunt directed harshly. 'I want Russell arrested!'

'What the hell for?' Russell demanded incredulously. 'I take my daughter out for the day, and——' The fierceness of his mother's expression silenced him. 'Ask Willow,' he muttered.

'I don't need to ask anyone about you, Russell, I've always known,' Simone said heavily. 'Your father was right, we spoilt you as a child, so much so that by the time you were an adult you believed you could have anything—or anyone—you wanted.'

'I don't know what you're talking about.' He shook his head derisively. 'I think there must have been some sort of misunderstanding. Willow, tell them that I had your permission to take Dani out for the day.' His gaze was steely.

She met that gaze apprehensively, moistening her lips nervously. 'I——'

'No!' Jordan's harsh interruption silenced her as he moved forward to put his arm protectively about her shoulders. 'You aren't going to intimidate her ever again,' he bit out grimly. 'We all know you took Dani without Willow's knowledge.'

'Willow?' Those cold blue eyes looked at her steadily.

Jordan's arm tightened about her shoulders, a promise in his eyes as he looked down at her tenderly. 'Willow, you never have to be afraid of him again,' he assured her gently. 'I'll take care of you and Dani. Always.'

Russell's mouth twisted. 'Isn't that rather a rash promise to make—to the woman *I'm* going to marry?'

'I wouldn't let her remarry you even if I believed

she actually returned your distorted version of love,' Jordan told him scathingly. 'Which I know she doesn't.'

'Willow is going to marry me,' Russell bit out. 'Aren't you, my darling?'

She gave an involuntary shudder at the endearment. But she didn't doubt for one moment that Jordan would protect her and Dani, she knew he hadn't made the promise rashly. Just as she knew she had misjudged his feelings earlier when he had left so abruptly. But did he mean anything more than just his promise? She needed him, not just to look after her and Dani, but to love her too.

She turned to Russell, her back very straight. 'I've already told you I won't marry you,' she said quietly. 'Nothing has happened to change my mind.' She looked at him defiantly.

'No?'

'No!' Willow and Jordan both answered the challenge at the same time, Willow looking uncertainly at Jordan as he stood stiffly at her side.

'Russell, when your father said Willow had told us everything, he meant everything.' Surprisingly Simone was the one to continue. 'We know what you did to her five years ago, and how you've treated her since,' she carried on remorselessly. 'As far as I'm concerned, I no longer have a son called Russell.' She turned away. 'David, call the police and tell them we have the person who kidnapped Dani.'

'Mother, no!' Russell sprang in front of her, his expression one of pleading. 'I don't know what

Willow has told you, but I'm sure it's all lies. She——'

His mother looked at him with cold eyes. 'I called you an animal a short time ago; on consideration I believe that was an insult to the animal kingdom! You're compulsive and obsessive.'

'I loved her——'

'You don't know the meaning of the word!' Simone spat the words at him. 'I'm ashamed of you; I only now realise the wrong I did this child all these years.'

'That "child" is having an affair with Jordan——'

'He loves her,' Simone corrected harshly. 'And I believe she may finally have found some peace and happiness with him. I hope so,' she added with feeling.

'You're all so self-righteous, aren't you?' Russell scorned, dropping his act. 'OK, so I forced Willow into the pregnancy, into marriage, into living with me. She didn't do so badly out of it; she's rich and famous in her own right now.'

'You have no idea, do you?' Simone said pityingly. 'You've no conception of what you did to Willow.' She shook her head. 'You're totally without morals or conscience.'

'That may be,' he scorned. 'But I'm not stupid enough to stay here and calmly let you have me arrested.' His gaze swept scathingly over Willow as she still stood within the protective arc of Jordan's arm. 'I hope he makes you happy!'

One second he had been standing in the lounge with them, the next he was gone. Willow half-turned to the man who held her so gently against him. 'Jordan . . . ?'

He shook his head. 'Let him go. He won't get far.'

'But——'

'I am going to make you happy, Willow.' He turned her in his arms. 'I love you very much, and I want to marry you.'

She blushed as she looked uncomfortably at Simone and David.

'Don't mind us, my dear.' David's smile was tinged with sadness. 'Simone and I will go into the kitchen and I'll make us all a cup of tea.'

Willow shakily returned his smile. 'After your earlier effort, I'm not sure my tea-set can stand it!'

'Don't worry, I'll make it.' Simone roused herself, moving with her usual agility to kiss Willow on the cheek. 'Welcome to the family, my dear. I don't think I've ever said that to you before,' she realised with a frown. 'I know you can never forgive Russell for what he did to you; why should you?' she added bitterly. 'But please try to forgive me for the wrong I did you.'

'You couldn't have known.' Willow hugged the other woman impulsively.

Simone blinked back the tears as she turned to her husband. 'Well, come along, David,' she said with her old authority. 'Can't you see they want to be alone? We can call the police from the kitchen.'

Willow moved awkwardly across the other side

of the lounge once Simone and David had gone through to the other room. Jordan had said he loved her, and he obviously didn't despise her as she had first thought he did, but could he now be offering to marry her out of pity? She couldn't bear it if he had!

He watched her with wary eyes as she avoided him. 'I do love you, Willow,' he said softly.

'Do you?' She frowned.

'I realise that wasn't the way to tell you, but—I needed to tell you then, to take the pain and bewilderment out of your eyes.'

'You certainly did that!' She gave a rueful grimace of a smile.

'My God, when I think what you've suffered! I had to leave earlier because I couldn't bear to look at you, knowing how I'd failed you.' A look of cold anger crossed his face, a pulse beating in his clenched jaw.

'*You* failed me?' She shook her head in puzzlement.

'If I'd been kinder to you in the past you might have been able to confide in me,' he said grimly. 'Instead I insulted you.'

'I wouldn't have told you, Jordan,' she assured him quietly.

'You *might* have done! God, I wish I'd known before—was I gentle enough for you?' He looked at her with dark eyes.

'I didn't need gentleness from you,' she spoke huskily. 'I always knew you would never hurt me. That night with you—it was the first time I've ever known physical pleasure,' she added with a blush.

'Because you love me?' His expression was strained.

'I——'

'Before you answer that, let me—tell you something.' His eyes glowed with a feverish light. 'I fell in love with you when Russell brought you home as his wife. It's the truth, Willow,' he insisted at her disbelieving gasp. 'But you were married to my cousin, expecting his child; he so obviously loved you, and I despised myself for caring for a woman who seemed to have succeeded in doing to Russell what Claudia had failed to do to me. I convinced myself you were like her, grasping and ambitious, and when you left Russell after only eighteen months of marriage, and he made such a big settlement on you at the divorce, it only seemed to confirm my belief. I told myself the family—and I—were well rid of you. But when I knew you were coming to Jersey last week, I couldn't stay away from you.'

'Jordan, you don't have to tell me any of this——'

'I do if I need to convince you that I've loved you for a very long time and didn't make the admission out of pity or guilt, as you thought I did. I knew it,' he muttered as she gave a guilty blush. 'Willow, I loved you before I knew any of this. And I believe you love me.'

Her head went back challengingly, years of hiding her real emotions making her wary. 'Do you?'

'You wouldn't have come to me that night if you didn't. God, physical love was the last thing you wanted, and yet you needed it from me.'

Tears squeezed between her closed lashes. 'I do love you——'

'Oh, Willow——'

'But I can't marry you.' She shook her head.

'Why not?' he rasped. 'I want more than anything to take care of you and Dani.'

Willow turned away. 'That's the point, Jordan,' she sighed. 'No matter what happens after today, Russell will one day come back into my life, would always be a threat to our happiness, like a dark cloud that never went away. I've lived with that threat for five years now, and I wouldn't ask anyone to share it with me.'

'You aren't asking me; *I'm* telling you. We love each other, and we're going to be married. Russell may have done his best to ruin your life, but I intend to see that you never know another day's unhappiness.'

She couldn't help smiling at his arrogance. 'Is that an order—sir?'

Jordan ruefully returned her smile. 'Let me make you happy, Willow.' He took her in his arms. 'Make *me* happy,' he urged throatily, their lips almost touching.

'It won't be easy,' she weakened.

'They say nothing worthwhile ever is. And you're very worthwhile. Say yes, Willow. *Please!*'

She loved him; she couldn't doubt that he loved her in the same way, she could see his love in the dark velvet of his eyes. 'I—yes,' she said force-fully. 'Yes, I'll marry you.' She smiled at him tremulously.

'Darling!' His lips claimed hers moistly, search-ingly, the aching sweetness of the kiss telling her more surely than words how deeply this man loved her. 'We—— That will be the police, I expect.' He straightened as the doorbell rang, his eyes dark with concern. 'Just tell them the truth, darling, and—— What the hell?' He moved to the door as Simone let out a gasped cry.

A policeman stood just outside the door, Simone heavily supported by David as she sobbed quietly.

David turned to them with pained eyes. 'Russell's car skidded on some oil in the road and he collided with a truck. He's dead,' he told them dully.

'Darling, do stop fussing with your hair!' teased Jordan. 'No one is going to be looking at you anyway!'

'Thank you very much!' she scowled up at him, although the glow of love in her eyes belied her tone.

'Well, you've done your bit, sweetheart.' He sat on the side of the bed.

'Really?' she taunted. 'I can have this bedroom to myself in future, then, can I?'

'Oh no,' he laughed softly. 'I still need you.' He kissed her lingeringly on the lips. 'But Simone and David will just want to gaze at young Master

Justin over there.'

They both looked down indulgently at their day-old son as he slept unconcernedly in his crib beside the bed. Almost two years had past since the night Jordan had asked Willow to marry him. They had been good years, ecstatically happy years, for all of them. It had taken all of three months after the wedding for Dani to begin calling Jordan 'Daddy', because that was what she felt he was to her.

Russell's death had been a tragic release for Willow, although she felt for Simone and David at their loss, knowing the older couple were shattered. But they had slowly got over it, had visited Jordan and Willow at their London home, were even now waiting excitedly outside the bedroom for their first glimpse of their new 'grandson'.

Willow had insisted, to Jordan's chagrin, that the baby be born at home, although he had wholeheartedly approved when he was able to see the excitement in Dani's face when she visited her new brother only minutes after he had been born. Dani had stood gazing down at the red-faced infant with rapt attention before announcing in a very grown-up voice that he was 'beautiful'. She had then run off to tell Barbara, their friend and confidante, all about him. With Russell's death, Willow and Dani no longer needed protecting from him, but Barbara was so much a part of the family that she had stayed on to help with Dani and the new baby, and had soothed Jordan the night before when Willow's arrogantly assured husband had seemed about to collapse at the entrance of his son into the world.

Willow impulsively clasped his hand in hers, thankful that this wonderful man loved her, that they had found such happiness together. 'I love you,' she told him with feeling.

'I love you, too.' Brown velvet eyes slowly caressed her. 'Thank you for completing our family with Dani's brother.'

A family. She at last had a family whom she loved, and who loved her. Most of all she had Jordan. She needed nothing else.

Coming Next Month

Available in July wherever paperback books are sold, or through Harlequin Reader Service:

In the U.S.
901 Fuhrmann Blvd.
P.O. Box 1397
Buffalo, N.Y. 14240-1397

In Canada
P.O. Box 603
Fort Erie, Ontario
L2A 5X3

Take 4 books & a surprise gift FREE

SPECIAL LIMITED-TIME OFFER

Mail to   **Harlequin Reader Service®**

In the U.S.   In Canada
901 Fuhrmann Blvd.   P.O. Box 609
P.O. Box 1394   Fort Erie, Ontario
Buffalo, N.Y. 14240-1394   L2A 5X3

YES!   Please send me 4 free Harlequin Romance® novels
and my free surprise gift. Then send me 8 brand-new novels every
month as they come off the presses. Bill me at the low price of
$1.99 each*—an 11% saving off the retail price. There are no
shipping, handling or other hidden costs. There is no minimum
number of books I must purchase. I can always return a shipment
and cancel at any time. Even if I never buy another book from
Harlequin, the 4 free novels and the surprise gift are mine to keep
forever.   118 BPR BP7F

*Plus 89¢ postage and handling per shipment in Canada.

Name   (PLEASE PRINT)

Address   Apt. No.

City   State/Prov.   Zip/Postal Code

This offer is limited to one order per household and not valid to present
subscribers. Price is subject to change.   DOR-SUB-1D

Janet Dailey
Americana

A romantic tour of America with
Janet Dailey!

Enjoy two releases each month from this
collection of your favorite previously
published Janet Dailey titles, presented
alphabetically state by state.

Available NOW wherever paperback books
are sold.

All men wanted her,
but only one man would have her.

Desert Storm
Nan Ryan

Her cruel father had intended
Angie to marry a sinister cattle baron twice her age.
No one expected that she would fall in love with his
handsome, pleasure-loving cowboy son.

Theirs was a love no desert storm would quench.

Available in JUNE or reserve your copy for May shipping by sending your name,
address, zip or postal code along with a check or money order for $4.70 (in-
cludes 75 cents postage and handling) payable to Worldwide Library to:

In the U.S.

Worldwide Library
901 Fuhrmann Blvd.
Box 1325
Buffalo, NY 14269-1325
Please specify title with book order.

In Canada

Worldwide Library
P.O. Box 609
Fort Erie, Ontario
L2A 5X3

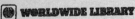 **WORLDWIDE LIBRARY**

STM-1

JULIE ELLIS

author of the bestselling
Rich Is Best rivals the likes of
Judith Krantz and Belva Plain with

THE ONLY SIN

It sweeps through the glamorous cities of Paris, London, New York and Hollywood. It captures life at the turn of the century and moves to the present day. *The Only Sin* is the triumphant story of Lilli Landau's rise to power, wealth and international fame in the sensational fast-paced world of cosmetics.

Carole Mortimer

Merlyn's Magic

She came to him from out of the storm and was drawn into his yearning arms—the tempestuous night held a magic all its own.

You've enjoyed Carole Mortimer's Harlequin Presents stories, and her previous bestseller, *Gypsy*.

Now, don't miss her latest, most exciting bestseller, *Merlyn's Magic*!

IN JULY

MERMG

For the millions who can't read
Give the Gift of Literacy

One out of five adults in North America
cannot read or write well enough
to fill out a job application
or understand the directions on a bottle of medicine.

**You can change all this by joining the fight
against illiteracy.**

For more information write to:
Contact, Box 81826, Lincoln, Neb. 68501
In the United States, call toll free: 800-228-3225

**The only degree you need
is a degree of caring**

LIT—A—1

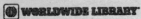